From the Files of

Madison Finn

Read all the books about Madison Finn!

Coming Soon!

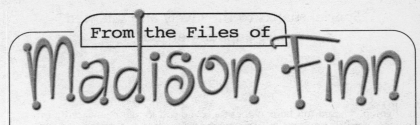

From the Files of Madison Finn

Double Dare

By Laura Dower

HYPERION
New York

For Nancy, Bryan, and Sarah in memory of John

**Special thanks to the lovely and talented
Lisa Papademetriou**

J Middle School

Text copyright © 2003 by Laura Dower

From the Files of Madison Finn and the Volo colophon are trademarks of Disney Enterprises, Inc. Volo® is a registered trademark of Disney Enterprises, Inc.

Printed in the United States of America

First Edition
3 5 7 9 10 8 6 4

The main body of text of this book is set in 13-point Frutiger Roman.

ISBN 0-7868-1736-4

Visit www.madisonfinn.com

Chapter 1

Madison Finn twisted the lock on her orange locker and tugged open the door. It was only September, but already books and papers were overflowing onto the floor. Her new American history textbook crashed down with a thud.

"Hey, Finnster!" a voice called out from behind.

Madison turned around to see Hart Jones standing there, smiling. Her heart raced.

Hart had once been the most annoying boy in her life. He had spent half of elementary school chasing her around with worms and other gross stuff. That was when he'd nicknamed her "the Finnster."

But now that they were both in seventh grade, something had changed. Hart had changed. This year, he was totally crushable. And Madison had fallen—hard—even if he did still call her by the same embarrassing nickname.

"Oops," Madison mumbled, leaning over to pick up the book. "I didn't mean to do that." Her cheeks purpled with embarrassment.

"Hey! Nice one, Maddie," someone else yelled from behind Hart.

Madison looked up to see her longtime friend Walter "Egg" Diaz leaning against the bank of lockers, mouthing off as usual. Next to him stood Chet Waters, a kid in their class whose family had moved to Far Hills from California the year before. He and Egg had been spending a lot of time together, and Madison had been spending a lot of time with Chet's twin sister, Fiona. The Waters family lived in a house just around the corner from Madison and her other best friend, Aimee Gillespie.

"Hey, you know what I think?" Egg asked.

Madison groaned. "No one cares what you think, Egg. . . ."

"Nice one!" Chet said.

"Yeah, whatever . . ." Egg cracked. "Well, I don't care what *you* think, Maddie." He turned and dragged Chet down the hall.

First period would be starting soon.

"I have to go, too," Hart said, waving a small good-bye to Madison. "Bye."

Madison thought she saw Hart's eyes twinkle

2

when he said good-bye. She watched his floppy brown hair bob down the hall.

"Yeah," she sighed. "So long."

Thankfully, Fiona and Aimee had not magically appeared to catch Madison at the scene of her crush. Neither BFF knew about Madison's *true* feelings for Hart. Although her first year of junior high had only just begun, Madison was having trouble figuring out her relationships with boys. The only friends who knew about Madison's undying love were her pug, Phineas T. Finn, and Bigwheels, her keypal—and both were sworn to secrecy.

Brrrrrrrrring.

Madison had to hurry. Computer class was upstairs, and she had to race to get there before the second bell rang. Quickly, she shoved her books into her bag, which was a super-tight squeeze, considering that she had her laptop computer stuffed in there, too. Madison carried her laptop everywhere these days. Organizing her life in top-secret computer files named for friends, enemies, and everything in between was the best way to keep track of her most private thoughts.

As Madison climbed the stairs and walked into the computer lab, she spied Egg sitting at a desk alongside his other good friend, Drew Maxwell. Egg and Drew glanced over, but without saying a word, Madison took a seat as far away as she could. Luckily, she thought, Hart and Chet weren't there.

The lab was a brightly lit, open space with yellow walls. Every computer had its own private "station," with a divider that moved back and forth so kids could work alone or with partners. Mrs. Wing had decorated the classroom bulletin boards with colorful charts and a giant black-and-white poster of Albert Einstein sticking out his tongue. On one wall, she'd posted a list of computer lab regulations.

1. STUDENTS SHOULD HAVE RESPECT FOR ALL EQUIPMENT, TABLES, AND COUNTERS.
2. STUDENTS SHOULD NOT HAVE GUM, FOOD, OR LIQUIDS NEAR ANY TERMINAL.
3. STUDENTS SHOULD SAVE ALL WORK ON A DATA DISK.

And on and on . . . Despite Mrs. Wing's long list of more than twenty boring rules, Madison knew that this teacher was one of the coolest in all of seventh grade. In the weeks since school had begun, Madison had felt more comfortable in this class than in any other on her schedule. Mrs. Wing hardly ever raised her voice and she wore interesting jewelry and clothes. Madison always noticed those. Today Mrs. Wing had on an electric-blue scarf and gold bangles that jangled every time she waved her hands in the air.

It wasn't only the teacher that made Madison love computer class—it was the lab itself. The room was filled with all *new* computers. The year before

Madison and her friends arrived, Far Hills Junior High had received a special grant allowing them to purchase equipment, printers, and scanners. They'd even hooked up a high-speed Internet connection and Web TV.

Brrrrrrrrring.

As soon as the second bell rang, a kid in the back row named Lance raised his hand.

"We covered keyboarding skills and all that, Mrs. Wing. When do we get to play games?" Lance asked, pointing to his monitor. "Is there a joystick around here?"

Everyone in the room laughed.

"Computer games? Get real!" Egg exclaimed. "We're in *school*. In case you hadn't noticed."

"Now, Walter, there is no need for that," Mrs. Wing interrupted. "The truth is, Lance, that we *are* going to be playing quite a few computer games here in class. They're just a little different from games you're used to playing. But before we start class, I want to call your attention to something else. . . ."

She walked over to a large bulletin board near the classroom exit and pointed to a large sign. Above a photo of a diagrammed computer keyboard, the sign read COMPUTER CONTEST! DESIGN A WEB PAGE! WIN GREAT PRIZES!

"Now, I realize this is very last minute," Mrs. Wing said. "But I stumbled across the contest in the newspaper and I just had to tell you about it. I can already see that we have some very talented computer students who could do very well—even in a rush. I didn't want you to miss this opportunity."

The deadline was only two weeks away.

"Design a Web page by the end of September?" a kid in the front row said. "That's like . . . totally impossible."

Egg sat back in his chair and grinned. Madison knew exactly what he was thinking. It was not impossible. Not for him.

"I think some of you could do it!" Mrs. Wing cheered. She read the poster aloud. "'Web-tastic Media Partners invites junior high school students to enter the seventh annual "I Can Do That!" Computer Contest. Create Web pages for great prizes! Open to pairs of students in seventh, eighth, and ninth grades.'"

The most exciting part of the contest was the prize list. Madison could read it from where she was sitting.

GRAND PRIZE: COMPUTER WITH ZIP DRIVE, CD BURNER, AND COLOR PRINTER!

FIRST PRIZE: $500 AND COMPUTER SOFTWARE AND ACCESSORIES!

SECOND PRIZE: $100 AND COMPUTER ACCESSORIES!

THIRD PRIZE: $50 AND ONE-YEAR SUBSCRIPTION TO *COMPUTER UNIVERSE*

"Is anyone interested?" Mrs. Wing asked. "It's a great opportunity for some of you to show off your computer skills. I'd like to see that myself!"

Madison turned her chair around to catch Egg's eye, but he wasn't looking in her direction. Drew didn't see her either, so she turned back to her desk, feet tapping impatiently. Class had only begun, but now Madison could hardly wait for it to be over. She had to speak to Egg—now. She had to get him to enter the contest with her.

Egg had been the first person to show Madison how to use a computer. He was the smarter-than-smart guy who went to computer camp every single summer—and bragged about everything new that he'd learned. With Egg on her side, Madison couldn't lose—not even with such a tight deadline.

The moment the first bell rang for the next class, Madison leaped out of her seat and stopped Egg before he left the computer lab.

"Hey!" Madison shouted. "Wait up!"

"What for?" Egg groaned. "You were dissing me at the lockers this morning."

Drew laughed.

"I was NOT dissing anyone," Madison said, trying to sound convincing. She moved around the two boys to block their exit route. "I was just goofing around."

"Look," Egg continued. "I have to get to science class. Could you move?"

"That contest Mrs. Wing was talking about sure sounds like a lot of fun," Madison said. "Don't you think?"

"Yeah. So?" Egg said.

"Well, I thought I'd ask you to be my partner," Madison said. "It makes sense, right? We're friends. We always play computers together. We can—"

"Sorry. I already have a partner," said Egg matter-of-factly.

"Oh," Madison replied, surprised. She glanced over at Drew.

"Don't look at me," Drew said, shaking his head.

"I'm doing the contest with Chet," Egg announced.

"But—" Madison started to say, but she cut herself off. Her insides were squirming.

"So what? It's not like this contest is a big deal or anything," Egg said. "Now, would you MOVE?"

"Yeah. No biggie," Madison said. She stepped out of Egg's path and let him pass.

"Chill out, Maddie," Egg added, hurrying out of the lab. "You'll find another partner."

Madison sighed.

"Are you okay?" Drew whispered. "You look a little . . . weird."

"I can't believe he did that," Madison said.

"Yeah, well . . ." Drew shrugged.

They stood there in silence for a few moments. Then Madison got an idea.

"Drew?" Madison asked. "I know I just asked Egg to be my partner and you were standing right here . . . and it's probably not too cool to be asking you second and not first . . . but do *you* have a partner for the contest?"

"Me?" Drew cleared his throat. "Well . . . yeah, actually I do."

"You do?" Madison gasped. She wanted to take back the question immediately.

"The thing is . . . we saw the contest posted up there yesterday," Drew admitted. "Me, Egg, and Chet. And those guys paired up right away, so I went ahead and asked this guy from my English class if he wanted—"

"Whatever," Madison said, picking up her orange bag. "I don't care."

"I'm really sorry, Maddie," Drew said.

"Whatever," Madison said again. His responses sounded like Egg's. Boys were all the same: LAME. Madison slunk out of the computer lab. She wondered if Egg and Drew's actions had given *her* bad karma for the contest?

She'd been rejected twice—and it wasn't even lunch yet.

"Well, Egg is just being a wiener," Aimee said when Madison spoke with her that night. Madison was sleeping over at Aimee's house for the week while her mom was away on a business trip in Paris, France.

She produced documentaries for her company, Budge Films, and was always busier than busy.

"A wiener?" Madison laughed out loud. It was a funny comment coming from someone whose entire family were vegetarians.

"Yeah, a wiener, not a winner. A real DOG!" Aimee added.

Madison was happy for the comic relief, but she needed more than Aimee's cheering up to get through this. She needed *real* advice on what to do next. How could she enter the computer contest without Egg? Who would she find as a partner with only two weeks to go? And how could she possibly win?

Madison distracted herself from thinking too much by rummaging through Aimee's closet. She needed to borrow an outfit for dinner, since her dad and his girlfriend, Stephanie, would be picking her up in an hour or so. Aimee lent Madison a peasant skirt (which looked great with Madison's yellow top) and ylang-ylang perfume (which made Phinnie sneeze when he smelled it).

After Madison got dressed, she went in search of the best advice she could find. She had some time to kill before Dad's arrival. Aimee was busy practicing some ballet moves in the basement, so with Mrs. Gillespie's permission, Madison hooked up her laptop to go online upstairs. She hoped to find her keypal, Bigwheels, hiding out in a chat room on bigfishbowl.com.

Madison had met Bigwheels on the Web site during the summer, and they'd connected right away. Even though her family lived all the way across the country in Washington State, Bigwheels had a lot in common with Madison. They met in chat rooms regularly—and e-mailed even more often than that. Madison even knew her real name—Victoria. They were both in seventh grade now, and Bigwheels always had great advice.

Madison clicked on NEW MAIL and started to type.

```
From: MadFinn
To: Bigwheels
Subject: Need Your HELP!
Date: Wed 13 Sept 4:36 PM
```
What's gnu? I have a few school dilemmas.

I was counting on my pal Egg to do this computer contest with me, but he bailed out. What do I say to him? I want to enter and win all this stuff, but I have no one to do it with. And not only that but I'm working on the school Web site as the elections coordinator, and I have way 2 much 2 do!!!

Mom is away again. I miss her sooo much. Do ur parents ever go anywhere? Mine are always super busy with work.

Send me some valuable advice like u always do, pleeez?

Yours till the water falls,

MadFinn

Before sending the e-mail, Madison marked it "priority" with a little red exclamation point. Everything was happening so fast—and Madison needed advice *faster* than fast.

After sending the e-mail, she opened a brand-new file.

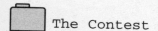 The Contest

Rude Awakening: Just when I think I can be a real winner, all my hopes byte the dust.

Why do I always over-think life? I can find another contest partner, can't I? With my luck, I'll probably end up with Lance the loser from the back row. Well, he's not exactly a loser, but I don't want to be part of his pair and that's that. Ugh.

Madison hit SAVE and contemplated her contest

fate. Phin pounced onto the edge of Aimee's trundle bed where Madison was sitting.

"What's happening, Phinnie?" Madison thought to herself, nuzzling his head. "It'll all work out, won't it?"

When Phin barked "Rowroooo!" on cue, Madison knew it would.

Chapter 2

Madison gazed up at the wipe-off board announcing Thursday's school lunch menu.

Meatball Loaf
Vegetable Lasagna Deluxe
Chicken-Fried Chicken
Salad Bar
Peas and Carrots
Mashed Potatoes
Lime Jell-O

"What's chicken-fried chicken?" Madison asked Fiona.

"I have *no* idea. Is chicken-fried chicken different from regular fried chicken?" Fiona replied.

"Forget that," Aimee said. "Have you ever heard of meatball loaf?"

Fiona giggled. "I'm getting a salad." She moved down the line with her cafeteria tray.

Gilda Z the Lunchroom Lady grinned at the girls as they passed by. "Try the lasagna, it's delish," she said, scooping some onto a plate.

Aimee grabbed the dish and kept moving. She hoped the vegetables would taste okay, even though what was on her plate looked more like rainbow mush. The three friends walked toward the back of the room where they'd scoped out "their" table since the start of school. It was bright orange—Madison's favorite color in the world.

The lunchroom was packed with seventh graders, including Madison's mortal enemy, "Poison" Ivy Daly. Since third grade, Madison had been shooting glares and swapping barbs with Ivy. Junior High had been even worse.

Ivy sat in the middle of the room at a yellow table with her drones, Rose and Joanie, a pair of girls who followed Ivy wherever she went. As they passed by, Aimee and Madison purposely looked away. But Fiona said a cheery hello.

Ivy smiled back. "Why don't you sit with us, Fiona?"

Aimee grabbed Fiona's elbow gently—and shot Ivy a look.

"Uh . . ." Fiona stammered, glancing over at Madison, who shook her head.

"What's your problem?" Madison asked Ivy.

"What's *yours*?" Ivy snapped.

"Fiona already has a place to sit," Aimee said with a sneer.

Fiona and her salad just kept on moving.

When the trio got to the back of the room, they were greeted by a bunch of boys flicking peas and carrots across the table. The lunchroom lady had stepped away, so no one would be caught for this particular lunchroom violation. Egg was in charge of the miniature vegetable shooting. Of course.

Just seeing Egg, Drew, and Chet together made her stomach flip-flop. Madison sat as far away from them as she could. Chet was laughing really loudly too, which made the whole scene even worse. He sounded like a siren.

"My brother is such a geek," Fiona whispered. "I don't know how I can possibly be related to him."

"Didn't you say your birthdays were coming up soon?" Aimee asked.

"Yeah, a reminder that we are twins," Fiona groaned. She rolled her eyes. "And it's not too exciting, believe me. We'll just do what we usually do. Eat a boring family dinner. Blow out the candles on a plain vanilla cake with chocolate-cream frosting. Try to keep sane as all my aunts and uncles call and ask the same things. Mom will buy us some dumb twin gift, like a matching outfit or something. She's been doing that since we were babies."

"That sounds kind of cool to me," Madison said. Since she was an only child with divorced parents, any kind of major "family" event sounded cool to her. She'd always wished for a brother or sister.

"I know what you mean about family events, Fiona," Aimee said. "I get so sick of my brothers when it's my birthday. They tease me a lot."

From the other end of the table, Chet let out another loud laugh. Fiona yelled at him to shut up, which got the entire table into a shouting match.

Madison stared off into space, watching and listening to everything like it was in slo-mo. She stared down at her slab of vegetable lasagna, which tasted like wet paper with tomato sauce, and turned once more to look at Ivy. Her enemy stood flipping her hair before a group of girls. Poison Ivy would figure out a way to create a winning Web page, Madison thought. If only—

"Maddie?" Fiona interrupted. "Are you entering that computer contest?"

"What?" Madison turned to Fiona, a little surprised. "What did you say?"

"My brother, Chet, told me about the contest last night. He told me that he's doing it with Egg. Like he even has a chance! I mean, it sounds way more like *your* thing than his—"

Madison smiled. "Thanks. I just wish I had someone to enter the contest with me."

Fiona grinned. "Um . . . *hello*?"

Aimee laughed out loud. "Yeah, Maddie. Duh. *Double* duh."

"What?" Madison cried, looking at her friends. She didn't know why they were teasing her.

"Think, Maddie," Aimee said. She motioned toward Fiona.

Madison bit her lip and looked over at Fiona. "Would you want to do it? I thought with soccer practice you wouldn't have time."

"It's true, soccer is my life," Fiona said, giggling. "But I still love computers!"

"Problem solved," Aimee said emphatically.

"Do you really want to enter . . . with me?" Madison said.

"Are you kidding? Chet keeps bragging about how he and Egg are going to win. I would love the chance to show him up. Ha!"

From across the table, Fiona made a face at her twin brother. He blew a raspberry back at her.

"Hey, Chet!" Fiona yelled. "Maddie and I were just talking, and I'm entering that computer contest too. SO THERE!"

Chet squinted back with disbelief. "What are you talking about, Fiona?"

"Since you and Egg went ahead and signed on together, Maddie and I are doing the same. And we're going to win."

Egg piped up. "You guys . . . uh, excuse me . . . *girls* don't have a chance."

"I can't believe you'd say that!" Madison gasped. She knew he was showing off in front of his friends.

"I dare you to enter," Egg teased. The other boys at the table laughed.

"You're so conceited, Egg," Madison said.

"I double-dare you!" Chet said, still laughing.

Aimee leaned over to Madison. "Why are you guys getting so worked up about this? It's just a dumb computer contest," she whispered.

Madison thought for a moment.

This was way more than just one contest. This was some kind of junior high ritual. It was a test of friendships. It was her chance to show Egg that he'd made a major mistake in not asking his oldest friend—her—to do the contest *first*.

"Aimee, a computer contest may sound dumb to you, but it really isn't dumb," Madison explained. "Not to me, anyway."

"So, Maddie, is it a dare or what?" Egg asked again.

Madison nodded. "Absolutely," she said, crossing her fingers under the table. Fiona and Chet were still screaming at each other, even though they could barely be heard above the sound of other voices, silverware, trays, and backpack zippers in the lunchroom.

For the remainder of the school day, Madison replayed the lunchroom exchange over and over in

19

her mind. When she arrived at Aimee's house later that night, Madison immediately turned on her laptop. She wanted to continue working on her file marked, "The Contest." Her mind swirled with thoughts. As always, Madison had to overthink everything. Had she done the right thing? Did she and Fiona *really* have a chance to win? Would this mean the end of her friendship with Egg?

An Insta-Message from bigfishbowl.com interrupted all the questions.

```
<Wetwinz>: You were soooo excellent
   in school! Meet me in private
   room COMPGIRL
```

Fiona was online. She wanted to talk—now. Madison scooted into the chat room.

```
<Wetwinz>: Chet is freaking
<MadFinn>: ?
<Wetwinz>: locked himself in his rm
   LOL
<MadFinn>: 1--)
<Wetwinz>: so what's the plan
<MadFinn>: plan?
<Wetwinz>: what do u wanna do for
   the Web page
<MadFinn>: IHNI
<Wetwinz>: I thought you had some big
   plan that's y I said I'd do it
```

<MadFinn>: LOL
<Wetwinz>: seriously
<MadFinn>: well I don't have a plan
    I only just found out about the
    contest
<Wetwinz>: what do the rules say??
<MadFinn>: the Web pg has to be
    like a homework helper
<Wetwinz>: what's that?
<MadFinn>: we nd to put lots of
    information and links
<Wetwinz>: IDGI
<MadFinn>: it's like a place to go
    for answers and cool information
    I think like a Web search
    function
<Wetwinz>: can we put a poll
    online? I always wanted to do
    that
<MadFinn>: I think you can download
    that from somewhere. what would
    the poll be about?
<Wetwinz>: something like what is ur
    fave subject
<MadFinn>: I saw a poll site once
    where kids put up notices on a
    bulletin board to vote for the
    hottest kid in their class
<Wetwinz>: weird
<MadFinn>: yeah and it got really
    nasty too people writing mean

```
      stuff about girls and guys in
      their class
<Wetwinz>: I could never do that
<MadFinn>: so what would OUR poll
      be?
```

Madison and Fiona chatted back and forth about different Web-page ideas, but neither of them could agree on a direction for the contest. They decided to meet over the weekend to finalize their plan. Fiona suggested that she spy on her brother so she could get information about what he was planning to do on the Web page with Egg. Madison wasn't sure that was fair, but then decided that *anything* seemed fair in this game.

And after all, it was a double dare.

When Fiona logged off, Madison headed into her e-mailbox. She had five spam messages, so she quickly deleted them. Bigwheels hadn't written back yet, so she popped off another quick e-mail to her. She needed the advice now more than ever.

```
From: MadFinn
To: Bigwheels
Subject: Fw: Need Your HELP!
Date: Thurs 14 Sept 5:02 PM
Did u get my last e-msg from
yesterday? I attached it again
below just in case.
```

Hey, I found a partner for the contest but now I am stuck figuring out what 2 do for it. My BFF Fiona is my partner. She is so nice but 4 this we're up against her brother so she is mad crazy to win, saying all this competitive stuff. It makes me a little nervous, like extra pressure to win. I think we do have a chance even though Egg is hands down the smartest guy in the contest. I would only admit that to you, BTW. If he knew I thought that he'd never let me forget it.
So do u have any brilliant ideas for us? Ur wicked good @ computers, I can tell. Once again, I need ur help.

SO . . . HELP!!!!!

Yours till the Web pages,

MadFinn

Chapter 3

The Contest

What a week! Fiona and I have been going bananas trying to figure out what to do for our Web page. We've had all these ideas, but it seems like everything we come up with is waaaaay too complicated. Like, I wanted to have a chat room, so people could discuss their homework. Good idea, right?

Wrong.

It's impossible to build, plus we'd need a 24-hour moderator . . . so that's out.

Fiona said we should have some funky graphics; maybe design our own stuff. But the software we'd need is seriously expensive. $300—on sale!

So now our list of a billion ideas = a

big zero. I wonder what Chet and Egg are doing? Fiona has been trying to pull some 007 on them, but she hasn't had much luck. Which is fine by me. Part of me doesn't even WANT to know what they're up to.

Rude Awakening: It's all fun and games until someone loses an eye—or a contest. I know winning isn't everything . . . it's just the only thing you can think about when you're losing!

I hope Bigwheels writes back soon. I need inspiration! We have to win! I can't take Egg's bragging for the rest of junior high. HELP!

"I don't know, Maddie," Madison's father's voice cut into her thoughts. "I think that this dinner might be a big *mis*-steak."

Madison sighed and placed her elbows on the kitchen table, cradling her chin in her hands.

"Not even a courtesy chuckle?" Dad asked from his place by the stove.

Madison gave him a lopsided smile. "Maybe if you didn't crack the same joke every time you made steak for dinner—"

"Hey," Dad protested, "when I get a good joke, I stick with it."

Madison laughed, happy to be hanging with Dad at his place. He'd just gotten back from a business trip, so Madison and Phin were staying with him instead of Aimee tonight. Whenever Madison stayed over, Dad acted like it was a special occasion. He was even making her favorite dinner—steak and french fries. And best of all, Madison had her father all to herself. Lately, Dad always wanted to hang out as a threesome with his girlfriend, Stephanie. Madison liked Stephanie—a lot. But, sometimes she wanted to be a Dad hog.

Dad flipped the steak, which let out an angry hiss. The delicious smell of grilled meat filled the kitchen and Madison's stomach let out a growl. "Will it be ready soon?" she asked eagerly.

"Yep," Dad replied. "Better clear the table."

Madison powered down her laptop and stuck it into her bag. Then she got out the place mats and set the small table that sat in the corner of the kitchen.

"Dinner is served," Dad said as he placed the plates on the table.

Madison took a fry and popped it into her mouth. "Mmm." Dad's fries always came out per-fect—extra-salty, just the way Madison liked them.

"Hey!" Dad protested, "wait for me to—ketch up!" He held out a bottle of Heinz ketchup as Madison rolled her eyes and shook her head.

"Hmm," Dad said as he settled into his seat. "That makes two no-laughs in a row. Is everything okay, sweetie?"

Madison sighed. Dad was so good at knowing how she was feeling. "It's just that Fiona and I entered this contest. We're supposed to design a

Web page . . . and it's a little harder than we thought it would be."

"Bit off more than you could chew, eh?" Dad asked as Madison bit into a piece of steak. That actually made Madison laugh a little, and for a minute she was busy trying to chew and laugh at the same time.

"Dad—I'm being serious!" Madison protested as soon as she had swallowed her piece of steak.

"I know, sweetie, I'm sorry." Dad looked sheepish. "But, hey—maybe I could help you with your project. I know a thing or two about Web sites, you know."

Madison grinned. "That would be great!" she said happily. After all, Dad worked for a start-up Web site. He knew a ton of stuff about setting up Web pages and making them work.

"So—" Dad said. "What kind of Web page are you building?"

"It's a homework-helper site," Madison explained. "It has to be something educational. Fiona and I want to make something that looks really cool—but the graphics we like best take forever to download. Some of them even crashed my computer."

"Hmm," Dad said, obviously thinking hard. He had paused with a french fry halfway to his mouth.

Madison smiled. "Are you going to eat that?" she asked, nodding at the fry.

"What? Oh, yeah." Dad put the fry in his mouth

and chewed. "It seems to me that the most important thing is to have a Web page that works," he
said finally. "If it's a homework helper, it's important
for it to be *helpful*."

"Right," Madison agreed. "That's one of the
things they said specifically in the rules. The winning
entries have to be functional. Design and style are
graded in separate categories. They don't count for
as many points." At her feet, Phin let out a low
whine and looked up, sniffing the air. Madison cut
off a tiny sliver of steak and slipped it to him.

"What you need is useful content, and lots of it,"
Dad went on. "If you want to have special effects—
like graphics and sound—just be sure that there's a
point to them."

Madison sighed. "The only problem is, I don't
know where to start!"

"Have you checked out any other homework-
helper Web sites?" Dad asked.

Madison's eyes grew wide. "Umm—no," she
admitted, slightly embarrassed that she hadn't
thought of something so obvious.

Dad grinned. "Maybe we should start there. Why
don't you pull out the laptop while I take care of the
dishes?"

Madison snatched the last two fries off her plate
as Dad cleared the table, popping one fry into her
mouth and tossing the other one to Phin. Then she
pulled out her laptop.

Dad had made the Web-page project sound like fun again.

After the dishes were done, Dad pulled his chair next to Madison. She typed "homework" into a search engine and waited for the number of searches to come up onscreen.

```
Search: HOMEWORK.
Total items found: 1,321,395.
```

"See?" Dad said. "There's plenty of stuff to look at. "

"I think I'll start with the top three," Madison said, clicking through to a site called hellohomework. It had a list of school subjects and a complex database, including an online atlas and encyclopedia.

"This page is outta site!" Dad said, winking.

Madison clicked through to look at the atlas. "They've got a ton of great stuff," she agreed, ignoring Dad's bad pun. "But we could never make anything this complicated."

"No," Dad said, sitting back in his chair. "But you could provide a link to this page."

"Oh—" Madison said. "Right!" She clicked back to the search engine and tried another site. This one was mostly science centered, and had detailed information on plants and animals. Madison added the link to FAVORITES and kept surfing while Dad scooped out dessert.

"Dad?" Madison called out. "I'm trying to use the search feature, but it doesn't work."

"Too much stuff on that page," Dad said, slurping a spoonful of ice cream. "It's real slow. That's a good example of what *not* to do."

"Oh," Madison said. She nodded and clicked to a different page with a scrolling list of books by different authors.

"I just can't wait to tell Fiona about all these sites!" Madison said.

"Why don't you give her a call?" Dad suggested.

"Yeah!" Madison snatched the cordless phone off the wall and punched in Fiona's number, grinning.

"Hello?" said a male voice on the other end of the phone line.

Madison's grin evaporated.

Chet!

Just say hi, Madison told herself. She opened her mouth, but she couldn't make any sound come out. She didn't want to speak to Fiona's brother under any circumstances. Before she realized what she was doing, Madison hung up with a slam.

Oh my gosh! Madison thought, the minute she'd clicked off the phone. Why did I just do that? She hoped the Waters family didn't have caller ID. Even though she was at Dad's, Chet still could figure out who had hung up on him!

"Wrong number?" Dad asked as he put their dessert bowls into the dishwasher.

"Um . . . yeah," Madison lied. "I guess I'll just call Fiona later." She bit her lip, wondering why she'd hung up the phone like that. She felt a little more competitive about this contest than she thought she would feel when it began.

"It's getting late, Maddie," Dad said. "And you have school tomorrow. You should probably start getting ready for bed."

"Can't I just surf a little more?" Madison pleaded.

"Aren't you getting key-bored?" Dad asked.

Madison gave a half-laugh, half-groan. "I just want to check my e-mail," she pleaded. "Really, really quickly."

"Okay, okay." Dad relented. "You can have another fifteen minutes."

Madison liked bargaining with Dad for more bedtime. Mom never sent her to sleep on the clock at home, so why should she have to do that here?

Madison decided to Insta-Message Fiona rather than risk calling and getting Chet again. She logged into bigfishbowl.com and checked her buddy list.

Fiona wasn't online. But Chet *was*.

"Grrrrrr!" Madison fumed to herself. Why did Chet have to be such a phone and computer hog? Didn't he know Fiona and Madison had work to do?

Since the phone and IM were offline, Madison decided to send Fiona e-mail. She opened her e-mailbox and discovered a bunch of messages.

From: Bigwheels
To: MadFinn
Subject: Fw: Need Your HELP!
Date: Thurs 21 Sept 7:21 PM

Sorry I haven't written--u'll never believe what happened. My computer totally died! I was surfing the Web for info for an English project, and the screen went blank. Can you believe it? My mom was on the phone with the tech people for an hour, but nothing worked. They said we should send the computer to them and they could get it back to me in a month (!), but my dad said that the computer was way old anyway. It was going to cost too much to fix it, so we decided I should get a new one (!!!!!)

So I'm writing you from my (drumroll PLEASE) cool new laptop. And it's orange, which makes me think of u. We're practically twins now! The laptop is superfast, too, so I'm sure I'll be spending even MORE time online.

I don't have any brilliant ideas about ur Web page, but if I come across anything that looks

interesting, I'll totally share.
But don't worry! Ur so good with
computers--I know u and Fiona will
do great.

Yours till the cyber spaces,

Bigwheels a/k/a Victoria

Madison smiled and reached down to pet Phin. He was lying on his back, wiggling, making happy snuffling noises as Madison rubbed his belly. "Are you going to help me, Phinnie?" Madison asked.

"Rowrrooo!" Phin howled. He scooted around on his back, legs pumping the air. He looked so silly.

Madison felt the same way. But she remembered what her Gramma Helen always said: "The best way to get help is to ask for it." She had Fiona, Dad, and Bigwheels to ask. Madison could get all the help she needed—and make sure that her Web page would rate A+++ . . . right?

Bah-ling!

Madison's computer chirped and flashed.

Another new e-mail?

The newest message downloaded, and Madison read the address: Waters@bigfishbowl.com. Her heart skipped a beat. Was this from Chet—telling her that he knew she was the one who hung up on him? Madison clicked the message icon to find out.

```
From: Waters
To: MadFinn, Balletgrl
Subject: Fiona and Chet Birthday
Date: Thurs 21 Sept 9:17 PM
```
Hello, Madison and Aimee.

Fiona and Chet have a birthday
coming up, and I was hoping you
would help me! I want to plan a
surprise party for them. Usually I
have a special dinner just for
family, but I thought that it might
be fun to include some of Chet's
and Fiona's friends this year. Would
you help me make up a guest list
and send out an invitation?

Many thanks in advance! I will send
you another e-mail soon. Write me
back at this address.

Emily Waters (Fiona's mom!)

"Five more minutes, Maddie," Dad called from the other room.

"Okay," Madison replied, her eyes still glued to the screen. Madison couldn't believe it—Mrs. Waters wanted help planning a surprise party for Fiona? Of course Madison was in! She hit REPLY and wrote to Mrs. Waters, letting her know that she could definitely count on Madison's help. Then she for-warded the message to Aimee with a note saying, "Did you see this? Meet me before school—we need to chat!"

Unfortunately, Madison was so busy writing to Bigwheels and getting in touch with Aimee that she never had the chance to write to Fiona about what she'd found on the Internet for their Web-page project. Could she wait ten more hours until school started to tell Fiona the big news?

Phin jumped up on her leg so Madison could rub his ears.

"Good doggie," she cooed, shutting down her laptop. Madison and Phin disappeared into her room at Dad's apartment to get ready for bed.

Tomorrow was a big day and Madison needed her ZZZZs.

Chapter 4

Aimee was waiting by the school lobby when Dad dropped off Madison. As soon as Madison got out of Dad's car, Aimee rushed over, talking faster than fast.

"Oh, my god—OH, MY GOD—I have been up all night! Can you believe that Mrs. Waters actually wants us to help plan a surprise party for Fiona? Isn't that the best?" Aimee ranted breathlessly. "How exciting is this? I just love being part of a secret, especially when it's a cool one. What should the invitation look like? What should I wear? Do you think we should—"

"Whoa, whoa," Madison giggled. Her BFF could talk a mile a minute when she got going. "Slow down. I think the first thing we need to do is figure out who to invite."

"The guest list!" Aimee did a quick pirouette—

something she did often when she was excited. "Okay—who do we want to come, besides you and me?"

"And Fiona," Madison said, yanking open her lock.

"Right," Aimee agreed.

"I don't know," Madison said as she pulled her books from her orange backpack and dumped them into her locker. "I mean, the party is for Chet, too. Do you think we should just invite the whole grade?"

Aimee's blue eyes grew wide. "Ugh—no way! I hate huge parties. Let's just stick to our friends."

"Well . . ." Madison hesitated. Even though Fiona was new at school, Madison knew that she was friendly with a lot of people in their grade. And Chet was pretty popular, too. Madison and Aimee had promised to come up with a good guest list for the twins' party, not just a list of people *they* liked.

"Fiona and Chet have a lot of friends, you know," Madison said aloud.

"Yeah, but there's a short list. Fiona is best friends with you and me," Aimee said, doing a quick dance step. "And Chet is best friends with Drew and Egg. End of story."

"Huh?" Madison bit her lip. "Chet is also friends with Dan. And sometimes he hangs out with other guys . . . you know . . . like, um, Hart."

Madison said Hart's name as coolly as she could, but she could feel her face burning.

"And Fiona is friends with Lindsay. . . ." Madison added quickly.

Aimee shrugged. "True," she admitted. "Okay, this is going to take some thought, and we only have two minutes till first bell. Why don't you and I meet this weekend to discuss the party?"

"What party?" someone said. Madison jumped.

"Fiona!" Aimee squealed. "Hi! How's it going? Is that a new shirt? You look so great in green!"

Fiona started to laugh. "Thanks, Aim. Did you drink coffee or something?"

Madison put a hand on her chest as though to keep her heart from racing too fast as she came face-to-face with Fiona. Her mouth was a little dry. How much had she heard?

"H-h-hey," Madison stammered.

"You really do look great in green—don'tcha think, Maddie? I mean great!" Aimee said. She was babbling now.

"Aim, I've worn this shirt a thousand times," Fiona said. "But thanks, anyway. So—where's the party?"

Madison gaped at Aimee, silently pleading for help. She was no good at fibbing under pressure. How could they get out of *this* one?

Aimee kept right on talking. "Did you say 'party'? We were just talking about the VTV Ultimate Party Video countdown on Saturday. Do you want to come over and watch it with us?"

Fiona shook her head. "Sorry—I think I've got some family birthday stuff that night."

"Oh, right, Saturday's your birthday," Aimee said, pretending that Fiona's birthday had completely slipped her mind. Aimee nudged Madison with her elbow as if to say, "See how easy that was?"

"It's your birthday?" Madison croaked.

Fiona made a weird face. "Of course! I just told you about it the other day," she said. "I swear, Maddie, sometimes you can be such a space case!"

Brrriiiiing!

"Oh! There's the bell. I have to run to my locker," Fiona said. "See you guys later, okay?"

"See you!" Aimee called out. She turned to Madison. "Whew!" she said in a low voice. "That was close. Remind me never to let you work for the CIA."

"ME?" Madison said. "I don't even think the VTV Video countdown exists."

"Well, she bought it, didn't she?" Aimee said.

Madison pulled a red notebook from her locker and shut it with a bang. "And Fiona thinks *I'm* a space case!"

"I can't wait to tell Mrs. Wing all about our ideas," Fiona said as she and Madison walked down the hall toward the computer lab during their free period. Madison filled her friend in on everything Dad had said and what she had discovered while surfing the Internet the night before.

"She'll be able to help us pull it all together," Madison said.

But when Madison pulled open the heavy door to the computer lab, she got a shock. The room was packed! Was everyone in the seventh grade inside?

Mrs. Wing stood in the far corner, behind Ben Buckley. When she saw Madison and Fiona, she waved them over.

"Girls!" Mrs. Wing called. "Come take a look!"

Ben had the school Web site up on his screen.

"It's looking fantastic, Madison," Mrs. Wing said enthusiastically. "All of your hard work has paid off so far. Ben's just adding some finishing touches . . . see?"

Ben clicked on a link that listed homework assignments. "Even *I* think it looks pretty good," he said.

Madison rolled her eyes. Ben was one of the smartest guys in school, but he could be a royal pain.

"I just wanted to show you, and to say thank you for all your help," Mrs. Wing went on. "I know it's only been a few weeks, but I never expected we'd have this much done."

"You're welcome," Madison said happily. Helping Mrs. Wing with the Web site was fun. Madison loved to feel that she was helping to do something important for the school.

"Are you two here to work on your Web page?" Mrs. Wing asked.

"Yes," Fiona said. "Madison had some great ideas about linking to other Web sites."

"That's good!" Mrs. Wing said, smiling so her dark eyes crinkled at the corners. "As long as you follow the rules. Linked sites have to be useful and functional."

"Of course," Madison said. Fiona nodded, too.

"It's always best to play by the rules," Mrs. Wing said. "When it comes to contests, anyway."

"We were hoping that we could get on a computer and start working this afternoon," Madison said as she looked around the crowded room.

"As you can see, you aren't the only ones who hatched that plan." Mrs. Wing gave them another smile. "But it looks like there are two seats in the corner, next to Daisy and Heather. I'm making my way around the room to help everyone. Holler if you need me."

"Thanks, Mrs. Wing," Madison said. She skipped over to the computer in the corner and hit the power button.

"Hey, Daisy," Fiona said as she slid into a seat in between Madison and Daisy Espinoza, who played right wing on Fiona's soccer team.

"Hi, guys," Daisy replied. "Are you working on your Web page? Take a look at ours. Heather is so good at this."

"Mm-hmm," Madison said as she took a quick look at their computer screen. Daisy and her partner, a quiet girl named Heather Benyon, had already built a good portion of their page with a few short articles, including one on sports from around the world—for gym class, of course! It wasn't fancy, but it was farther along than Madison and Fiona's page.

Way farther along.

Another student, Montrell Morris, leaned back to peer at Daisy's screen, too. "Your page is okay," he said, pretending to yawn. "If you're into home-work."

Madison cocked an eyebrow. "I thought that was what we were *supposed* to be doing," she said, "making a useful educational page."

Montrell gestured to his computer screen. "Oh, I'm making something useful, all right," he said. "Mine has a program that randomly generates excuses for *not* doing your homework."

Madison laughed. Montrell was a real crack-up. She wasn't sure that the judges would love his idea, but at least he had a shot at the Most Original cate-gory—if there was one.

Madison and Fiona sat down in front of their own terminal and logged online. Fiona found a few new sites that Madison hadn't seen the night before. Working quickly, they captured the links and coded them for their Web page. Fiona even found a Web site that had free clip art.

"This is easy," Madison said as she downloaded an image of a wizard in a tall pointed hat. "He can be our homework magician." She typed in a line for their science page.

```
Finding science facts is a simple
trick—just point to the magician
and double-click!
```

Fiona giggled. "I have one," she said, leaning over to reach the keyboard. She quickly downloaded a cartoon of a cockroach and typed:

```
Don't let social studies be a pest—
click the bug for help that's best!
```

Fiona and Madison were working so intently that they didn't hear footsteps sneaking up behind them. "Whatcha doin'?"

Fiona let out a little shriek. Madison whipped around. Chet was standing right there . . . with Egg.

"You doofus!" Fiona yelled at her brother. "Don't you know better than to sneak up on people?"

Chet sneered. "What are you talking about?" he asked. "It's a free classroom. I can sneak wherever I want."

Fiona moved her body to block his view of the computer screen. "Quit trying to look at our Web page."

"Oh, puh-leeez," Chet said, rolling his eyes. "Like we want to see your lame Beanie Babies Fan Club page."

"And what have you done for *your* page?" Fiona shot back. "Let me guess . . . *nothing*?"

Chet folded his arms across his chest. "As if I'm going to tell you."

"Right," Fiona said, "because there's nothing to tell."

Madison looked over at Egg, who gave her a half-smile and shrugged. There was no point in trying to jump in when Chet and Fiona got into their sparring matches. You just had to wait until it blew over.

"So . . ." Egg said weakly. "How's it going, Maddie?"

"Okay, I guess," she said.

"Chet!" Fiona kept arguing, "Not only does your page stink, but so do your feet."

"Oh, good one, Fiona. Well, my feet don't stink as much as—"

"Don't even say it," Fiona wailed.

Madison turned away, trying not to listen.

"So how are *you*, Egg?" Madison said. She felt so awkward. Egg was supposed to be her best guy friend—but she could barely think of anything to say to him. She'd felt this way ever since he hadn't picked her as his contest partner.

"Good, I guess," Egg grunted. He shifted from one foot to the other.

Madison sighed. Fiona and Chet were still going at it.

"If that's the way you feel about it, then FINE!"

Chet said. "Egg and I will work on the other side of the room."

"Great," Fiona shot back. "It'll be easier to concentrate if I don't have to look at your ugly face, anyway."

"Come on, Egg." Chet started walking away.

"Bye, you guys . . . I mean girls," Egg said.

As the boys walked away, Fiona sighed. "Why in the world does Walter hang out with a grade-A nerd like my brother?" she grumbled. Fiona almost always used Egg's real first name.

"Egg can be a nerd, too, sometimes," Madison replied. "Believe me."

"No way," Fiona whispered, smiling a little. "He's a nice guy."

Madison stared straight ahead. Nice guy? Of course, Fiona would say that. Madison knew that Fiona had a serious crush on Egg and wouldn't say anything bad about him.

The Web-page contest was getting more complicated by the minute.

As the bell rang and free period ended, kids filed out of the computer lab.

"Coming to soccer practice today?" Daisy asked Fiona as she packed up her book bag.

"Yeah—I'll walk with you," Fiona said. "Just a sec." She turned to Madison. "Maddie, can we get together over the weekend and do some more work?"

"Sure," Madison agreed. "Call me—or e-mail me."

As Fiona walked away, Madison made a mental note to invite Daisy to the birthday party. And Egg. He belonged on the A-list, too.

Even if he was a traitor.

"Mom!" Madison called as she walked in the front door of her house.

There was a slight jingle as Phin bounced into the room and jumped up onto Madison's legs.

"I see Dad brought you home this morning," Madison said as she leaned down to pet him on the head. He wheezed hello.

"Maddie?" Mom said as she walked out of her office. The minute she saw Madison, her eyes lit up with a bright smile and she held out her arms. "Hey, honey bear. I missed you!"

Madison rushed into them and gave Mom an enormous squeeze. "I'm so glad you're home!" she said.

"Me, too," Mom said. "Paris was nice, but I missed you so much. Did you have fun at Aimee's and with Dad?"

"Tons," Madison said. "Mrs. Gillespie was super nice, as always. And Dad helped me with the Web page Fiona and I are building."

"Oh, Fiona's your partner?" Mom said. "See? I'm glad that worked out." Madison had filled her in on all the details the night before.

"Yeah," Madison agreed. "And guess what? Next weekend is Fiona's birthday, and Mrs. Waters asked me and Aimee to help her plan the party."

"I know!" Mom said. "Fiona's mom just called. Have you and Aimee made up the guest list yet? She wanted to know. The invitations need to go out as soon as possible."

"We started," Madison said. "We're going to finish working on it this weekend."

"What ideas do you have for the invitations?" Mom asked. "I bet you two could do some really neat things on the computer—you could scan in photos of the twins, or maybe cut some pictures out of magazines. That's your specialty."

Madison's eyes got wide. "I have an even better idea!" she said. "We'll send an e-vite!"

Mom smiled. "Now, *that's* a great idea."

"I just wish we could figure out who to ask," Madison said. "Aimee wants to keep it small—just us, Drew, and Egg. But I think we should invite a few more people."

"Just remember that it's a party for Fiona and Chet—not for you and Aimee. You should be inviting *their* friends, not just yours."

Madison sighed. "You're right, Mom," she said. "I'll talk to Aimee about it."

Mom kissed the top of Madison's head and disappeared back into her office. She came out with a take-out menu from Little China.

"I would love to order in tonight," Mom said. "Is that okay with you?"

Madison smiled. "Cold noodles with sesame sauce, please," she said. They tasted just like peanut butter, one of Madison's favorite treats.

"Chinese food it is!" Mom said, heading to the phone to call in the order.

Madison sat herself down at the table and picked up a pen. She scribbled around the edges of the Chinese menu.

English paper on Lois Lowry?
Web page contest?
Party invitations to _____?

Word by word, her doodles turned into a to-doodle list.

Madison scratched her head.

The weekend hadn't even begun and already she was busier than busy.

Chapter 5

```
<Balletgrl>: Maddie?
<MadFinn>: YRU up so early?
<Balletgrl>: early dance class. U?
<MadFinn>: thinking about Fiona's
    party. Mrs. Waters needs the
    guest list ASAP
<Balletgrl>: OK--you, me, Fiona
<MadFinn>: Chet, Egg, Drew who else?
```

Madison leaned back in her chair and stared at the cursor as it blinked on her computer screen. She was glad that Aimee had logged onto bigfishbowl.com so early on a Saturday. Hopefully, Fiona wasn't up and surfing the net yet.

```
<Balletgrl>: no clue. Sarah mileikis?
```

```
<MadFinn>: X-S
<Balletgrl>: girl in my ballet
   class. I know F would like her
<MadFinn>: hmm—this is F's birthday
   party, tho. SB for HER friends
<Balletgrl>: true. OK. yesterday U
   said Lindsay Frost. NE1 else?
```

Biting her lip, Madison looked down at the list she had scribbled on her notebook the night before. On it were the names of a few of the people she knew Fiona and Chet were friendly with.

```
<MadFinn>: Dan, Hart
```

Madison hoped that Hart's name looked casual there, right next to Dan's. She held her breath as she waited for Aimee's reply.

```
<Balletgrl>: OK
```

Madison let out the breath and smiled. She glanced at the other names on her list.

```
<MadFinn>: Suresh, Ben Buckley
<Balletgrl>: yes, no
<MadFinn>: Y not Ben?
<Balletgrl>: he's ok looking but WAY
   2 obnoxious! NE way, now we have
   too many boys. How about Beth?
```

```
<MadFinn>: Dunfey? Does she really
    talk to Fiona?
<Balletgrl>: Hmm. Does she really
    talk at all?
<MadFinn>: OK she's a no. Daisy?
<Balletgrl>: good 1
```

Madison's hands paused over the keyboard. She typed in the one person's name she *really* wasn't sure about.

```
<MadFinn>: Ivy?
<Balletgrl>: 1-)
<MadFinn>: I'm serious
<Balletgrl>: NEVER!
<MadFinn>: Fiona is sort of friends
    with her, and Chet too
<Balletgrl>: So that means we have
    to suffer?
<MadFinn>: this is for them, not us
<Balletgrl>: Ugh. Y do U always
    have to DTRT?
<MadFinn>: So she's on the list
    then?
<Balletgrl>: Fine
<MadFinn>: What about Joan and Rose?
<Balletgrl>: THE DRONES? Do we have
    a choice? But if they act like
    snobs, YOYO
```

Madison laughed, relieved that she and Aimee

had agreed on the guest list so quickly. She had expected more disagreements from her BFF. As Madison started to type in another question for Aimee, her computer bleeped.

Insta-Message.

```
<Wetwinz>: RU there?
```

Madison nearly toppled out of her chair. Fiona was online? Madison had to get out of the chat room with Aimee right away! If Fiona joined, the surprise party would be ruined.

```
<MadFinn>: GTG! Fiona's online!
<Balletgrl>: TTYL! *poof*
```

Madison breathed a sigh of relief, then replied to Fiona's Insta-Message.

```
<MadFinn>: hey Fiona im here
<Wetwinz>: RU coming over? When?
<MadFinn>: ASAP. found some cool new
    graphics for our page.
<Wetwinz>: great. The computer is
    ready & waiting. CUL8R!
```

Phin lifted his head sleepily as Madison slipped her feet into a pair of comfortable black suede clogs.

"Go back to your nap, Phinnie," Madison whispered, as she shoved her notebook into her orange book bag. She ran a quick hand over his fur and walked out the door.

"Where are you headed?" Mom asked as Madison walked into the kitchen.

"Over to Fiona's," Madison said swiping an apple from the bowl on the table. "I'll be home by three."

"Okay," Mom said absently. She sipped her coffee and looked back at her paper. It always took Mom a long time to wake up on weekends.

Madison walked the one block to Fiona's house quickly, her mind consumed by the Web page and party planning.

The minute she rang Fiona's doorbell, Madison heard footsteps running down the stairs. Fiona pulled open the door, breathless.

"Maddie!" Fiona said as she pulled Madison inside. "I'm so glad you're here! Mom and Dad are out playing tennis, and Chet is over at Egg's. We've got the whole house to ourselves!"

"Wow!" Madison said, relieved that she wouldn't have to see Chet. It was going to be hard enough to keep the party secret from Fiona, without having to worry about her brother, too.

"The computer is in here," Fiona said as she led the way through the first floor of her immaculate house toward her Dad's study. Madison was always amazed at how neat everything was at Fiona's place.

Madison's mom always said that their own house looked "lived in," which was a nice way of saying that she, Madison, and Phinnie weren't exactly the world's greatest housekeepers.

Madison had written down the names of a few more free graphics sites in her small wire-bound notebook. She pulled the notebook out of her backpack and put it on the desk while Fiona booted up the computer.

Madison bent over and reached into her bag for a pen.

"What's this?" Fiona asked.

Madison's heart stopped. She lifted her head to see what Fiona was looking at. The notebook was open to the page with the list of people to invite to Fiona and Chet's party.

Fiona read the list aloud. "Chet, Egg, Daisy . . ." She looked up at Madison. "What is this? A list of our competition for the Web-page contest?"

Madison gasped for breath. "Uh, yeah," she lied. "I was trying to think of anyone who might have a better shot at winning the contest than we do. How did you guess?"

"I think you can scratch Hart Jones's name off the list," Fiona replied. "I don't even think he's entered the contest."

"Good point," Madison said. She leaned over and scratched his name off the list. Fiona wasn't even suspicious?

"Okay, work time!" Fiona turned back to the computer. "We'll size up the competition later."

Madison laughed to herself. Fiona really didn't have a clue! She watched as Fiona typed in a Web address of a graphics site. Its home page appeared.

"Out of the chair," Chet said, barging into the room. "Egg and I need the computer."

"What are YOU doing here?" Fiona barked. Then she turned to Egg and changed her tone completely. "Hello, Walter," she said sweetly.

"Hi," Egg said to the room.

"Out of the chair," Chet repeated, shaking the back of the chair Fiona was sitting in. "You've had your turn. Move it."

"We just started!" Fiona protested. "Besides, I thought that you were going to work at Egg's place."

"My mom needed the computer," Egg explained.

"Our connection is faster, anyway," Chet said.

Fiona glared at her brother. "Connect this!" she said, holding up her fist.

Chet grabbed her forearm and wrestled her out of the chair. Egg and Madison stood back.

"Chet!" Fiona squealed. "STOP IT!"

"It's not like you guys are doing anything useful," Chet went on. "No one is going to want to read your History of Hair Clips Web page."

Madison stepped in. "We are *not* doing a page on the history of hair clips," she said.

"What *are* you doing, Maddie?" Egg asked. It was the first words he'd said directly to her. Was he teasing or just being annoying? Madison couldn't tell from the half-smile on his face.

"Uh—" Madison started to respond. She looked at Fiona, who shook her head. "Our Web page is none of your business, Egg," Madison said.

"Sor-*ry*," Egg huffed. "Can't you take a joke?"

"You're the JOKE," Madison said.

Chet let out a loud laugh, but Madison felt a pang of guilt. She sounded so harsh. Where had those words come from?

"Nice 'tude, Maddie," Egg said.

"Well, what are *you* guys doing?" Madison asked, trying to act nicer.

"Like I'm going to tell you," Egg said.

"They're probably making a program that shows you how to pick out nail polish colors," Chet joked.

"We wouldn't want to steal *your* idea," Fiona said dryly.

Chet glared at her. "Come on, Egg," he said. "Let's get out of here."

"That's the best idea you've had all day!" Fiona shouted as her brother and Egg walked out of the room. She ran behind them to shut the door.

"Way to go, Fiona!" Madison cheered. "You sure told him."

"Was I too harsh?" Fiona asked.

Madison chuckled. "I'm sure Chet will get over it."

"Chet? Who cares about Chet?" Fiona said. "I'm talking about *Walter*. Was I too rude? What does he think of me now?"

"Walter?" Madison said. "Fiona, you need to chill. Egg doesn't care—"

"Really?" Fiona asked. "Maddie, do you think there's a chance that Walter might like me?"

Madison raised her eyebrows. "Um . . . maybe if you stop calling him Walter."

Fiona stuck out her tongue and they both started to giggle.

"Do you really feel like working on the Web page anymore?" Fiona asked.

"Not really," Madison said.

"Me, neither." Fiona stood up. "Let's go up to my room and read some magazines." She cupped her hands around her mouth and yelled into the hall, "CHET! You can have the computer now! CHE-E-E-E-T!"

Madison held back a laugh.

"What's so funny now?" Fiona asked.

"Oh, nothing," Madison said. "It's just that— maybe life isn't so bad without brothers and sisters. I know I couldn't deal with a Chet in my house."

"Right, Maddie! Rub it in," Fiona said, joking around. She yelled out for her brother again, louder this time.

Madison covered her mouth to keep from laughing, again.

* * *

57

"Hi, Mom!" Madison said as she raced into her house later that afternoon.

"Madison, you're late," Mom said. "And you—"

"I know, Mom, I'm sorry," Madison said, zipping up the stairs. "But I lost track of time at Fiona's, and now I have to call Aimee right away!" She grabbed the cordless phone and took it upstairs.

Madison shrugged off her backpack and punched in Aimee's number.

"Hello, may I please speak to Aimee?" Madison asked as soon as she heard a voice at the other end of the line.

"Yo! I'm on the other line." It was Aimee's brother, Dean. "Is this Madison? I'll have Aimee call you when I'm done."

The phone clicked off.

Madison sighed with frustration. Dean was a notorious phone hog—she knew he wouldn't be off for hours. Besides, it was unlikely that he'd even give Aimee the message. Madison had to find another way to contact her friend.

Quickly, she booted up the computer and went to her e-mail box. There were three messages waiting.

FROM	SUBJECT
✉ Bigwheels	Re: Fw: Need Your HELP!
✉ Boop-Dee-Doop	Mega-Mambo-Sale
✉ JeffFinn	Surf City

Even though Madison was dying to hear what Bigwheels and Dad had to say, she forced herself to write to Aimee first, even adding an urgent exclamation point to the message.

From: MadFinn
To: Balletgrl
Subject: Gotta Party!
Date: Sat 23 Sept 4:13 PM

Aim, we HAVE to get working on Fiona's party!!!!! Mrs. Waters was walking up the sidewalk as I was leaving Fiona's this afternoon, and she asked me all of these questions about what we should do. Should we have games? What kind of decorations do we want? Do we just want to order pizza, or should we have something more special???

I had NOOOOO idea, so I said I'd ask u. So I'm asking. But we have to decide *soon* b/c the party is only a week away. Oh--and I almost told Mrs. W that we'd bake the cake but I wanted to wait & talk 2 u first.

This is going to be funner than fun!!!! Wait--is funner a word? (:-)

BTW--you'll never believe what
happened at Fiona's. Don't scream
but she saw the guest list!! Only
for a second--and she had no clue
what it was. Whew, right? I know
what ur thinking again, that I
can't work for the CIA. LOL.

How was ballet practice? WBS!!

Maddie

**Madison clicked SEND and eagerly returned to her
inbox, where messages from Bigwheels and Dad
were waiting.**

From: Bigwheels
To: MadFinn
Subject: Re: Fw: Need Your HELP!
Date: Sat 23 Sept 2:10 PM
I've been thinking about your Web
page, and I'm wondering whether
you'll be using any sound files
on your page? I found this cool
site--animalbytes--that has a sound
file for practically every animal on
the planet--you know, like a lion's
roar, an elephant's trumpet, a
giraffe's . . . well, whatever. You
can download the file onto your

computer, and upload it onto your
page. I thought it would be good
for science projects, stuff like
that.

Sorry this is so short. I'll write
L8R.

Yours till the rain forests,

Bigwheels

Madison was glad that Bigwheels was trying to
be helpful, but wasn't sure that sound files would
work for the Web-page contest. Was adding sound
too complicated?

I'll check out the site but stay simple, Madison
told herself as she filed the e-mail into her file called
THE CONTEST. At least for now.

She deleted the advertisement from Boop-Dee-
Doop; and then opened up the last e-mail . . . from Dad.

From: JeffFinn
To: MadFinn
Subject: Surf City
Date: Sat 23 Sept 4:57 PM

Hi Maddie! I found another site
that might be good for your contest
page. Check out bighomeworkfun.
You'll find a lot of great links.

BTW, What do you get when you cross a duck with a beach bum?

A Webbed surfer!

;-D

Dad

Madison typed the bighomeworkfun Web address into her browser and waited for the page to load. She couldn't believe all of the great help she was getting! This Web page was practically building itself . . . sort of. She clicked on an icon of a black-board and waited for the next page to open. It was a slow site.

"Maddie," Mom said from behind her. "You were late. And now you're playing around on the computer? It's time to take Phinnie for a walk."

"Okay, Mom," Madison replied without turning around. "In just a minute—"

"No." Mom's voice was firm. "Now."

Madison turned around and saw her mother frowning and holding Phin's leash. Phin looked up at Madison with his big puppy eyes.

"Rowrroooo," he wailed.

Madison grabbed the leash from Mom. "I'm sorry," she said. "I just lost track of time."

"You're forgiven, Honey Bear," Mom said with a smile. "But dinner is in half an hour, so get moving."

"Back in a flash," Madison promised as she hurried through the house with Phin. She grabbed a jacket from the peg in the front hallway and threw it on as they stepped onto the porch.

Phin strained at his leash, eager for his walk. "Okay, okay," Madison said. "I'm hurrying." She loped along, sucking in the fall air—still warm, but with just a hint of fall crispness to it. As she looked around, Madison saw that the neighborhood foliage was just starting to turn gold, orange, and red. The multicolored trees looked like monsters against a sky that was deepening from afternoon pink to evening purple. The sun was going down earlier now.

Madison thought about how quickly the seasons changed. . . .

Like a lot of things.

Egg popped into Madison's mind. He'd been one of her best friends forever. They'd always told each other everything since they were small. But in the last few days, things had definitely changed between them.

Along the sidewalk, someone had raked up a small pile of fallen leaves. Phin plunged in, scattering them everywhere. Madison tugged hard on his leash.

"No, Phinnie," she said. "We'd better leave those alone or else we'll be in trouble with the neighbors."

As they cruised along Fiona's block, Madison still couldn't get her friends out of her mind. Why did

Egg and Chet assume that Fiona and Madison's page would be bad? It hurt to hear them tease. *Hair clips* and *Beanie Babies?* HA! The boys were probably working on a page about shooting hoops and fart jokes.

Phin started chasing a runaway leaf down the street. Madison ran after him, pulled along by the leash, back toward home.

Madison was more determined than ever. She and Fiona would do everything in their power to make those boys eat their words. So what if Egg and Chet's double dare meant double the work? It could also mean double the fun!

Let the games begin.

Chapter 6

By the time Madison slid into her seat in Mrs. Wing's classroom on Monday afternoon, her head was spinning. She'd spent most of the weekend studying for Señora Diaz's Spanish vocabulary quiz and for a math test. Now that both were over, Madison finally had some downtime in the computer lab.

Madison found a terminal away from everyone else and connected to the Internet. Fiona wasn't alongside her, but the two had agreed to divide the work on their Web page. While Fiona was busy with the English, foreign language, and social studies part of their homework-helper page, Madison would work on science and math.

The search engine chugged and Madison awaited the results to her question: *What science and nature sites are the best?* Interesting sites popped up—like one called deepdeepblueseas—with pages of information on different marine animals, including sharks. Madison found pictures of sharks in their natural habitats that she copied onto a disk. *Even if I don't win the Web page contest,* Madison thought as she surfed through the site, *I definitely will kick butt on my next science paper.*

"Mrs. Wing?" someone yelled from across the room.

Madison looked up and saw the back of Egg's head. He was in a terminal on the other side of class, waving his hand eagerly in the air.

"I'll be there in just a minute, Walter," Mrs. Wing said. She turned back to Lance, the student she was helping first, and pointed to the screen.

"That link isn't working properly," Mrs. Wing told Lance. "Are you sure the HTML coding is right?"

"I've checked it a hundred times," he insisted.

"Let's take a look together," Mrs. Wing said, tucking a stray strand of hair behind her ear. She was wearing a red wrap dress and a necklace of large amber beads. Her hair was done up in a loose French twist. Madison knew that if *she* tried that hairdo, it would look like a mess. But on Mrs. Wing, it looked prettier than pretty.

"Mrs. Wing!" Ben Buckley also called out her name. "Can you help me please? It's an emergency!"

"Lance first, then Walter, then you," Mrs. Wing said as she leaned over and typed on Lance's keyboard. "And there's no need to shout, Ben. That goes for everyone in this room. I'll get around to *all* of you."

Madison smiled. She loved the way Mrs. Wing never hurried, and always gave whoever she was helping her undivided attention.

After turning back to her computer screen, Madison scrolled down the page layout she and Fiona had put together so far. A headline moved across the top like a theater marquee: WELCOME TO MADISON AND FIONA'S HOMEWORK CENTER. Below that were icons for each of the subjects they wanted to cover: English, social studies, science, and others. Madison plugged in the new shark image as the icon for science. Even though it *looked* exciting, she needed to jazz up the page in a different way.

More pictures? More special effects? What was the name of the sound-bite site Bigwheels had recommended?

Animalbytes! Madison remembered and typed in the address. As she browsed and clicked, Madison discovered every animal and nature sound imaginable—and they were all free. Downloading the sound files was way easier than she had thought. Madison could even use the sounds for other purposes, too.

Like the PARTY!

The day before, when Madison and Aimee had brainstormed the content and design for the surprise party e-vite, they were only thinking about the images and the words. What if Madison could figure out how to add sound to the invitation? She quickly surfed around in search of another sound site that would have the noise of a bowling ball knocking down pins in a bowling alley. With that noise and a little formatting, Madison would be ready to send the best multimedia e-vite ever.

"Mrs. Wing?" Egg yelled. His voice startled Madison.

"Please be patient, Walter, I'm coming," Mrs. Wing said.

But an impatient Egg kept clicking his mouse as if he wanted to squash a bug onscreen. What was his problem? Madison wondered. Egg seemed grouchier than grouchy. Maybe he's having trouble without Chet there to help?

WAIT! Madison thought. Why am I wracking my brain to figure this out? Egg will know how to add a sound to an e-vite! I should ask him!

The only trouble was that they weren't really talking.

There were only a few minutes left before the bell and the end of class. Deciding that now was her chance to break their silence and get Egg's undivided attention, Madison logged off and slipped out from behind her desk.

Egg saw her coming and scowled. "What are you looking at, Maddie?" he asked. "Trying to figure out what I'm doing for the computer contest?"

Madison rolled her eyes, but decided not to take

the bait. "Actually, I came over here to talk to you about something totally different," she said. "I have a secret and I could use your—"

"WHAT?" Egg snarled. He was still scowling, but he looked a little interested. "What?" he said again, nicer this time.

"You have to promise not to tell," Madison said.

"Fine, I promise," Egg said. "What?"

Madison leaned over and kept her voice low. "Mrs. Waters asked me and Aimee to help her plan a surprise party this Saturday for Fiona and Chet," she said. "And so we're making the electronic invitation."

Egg's eyebrows flew up. "Really?" he asked.

Madison nodded. "Yeah. Aimee and I came up with a list of people to invite for Fiona, but we don't really know who to invite for Chet. I thought maybe you could help. And I'd like to add sound to the e-vite, but I'm not really sure. . . ."

"Sure," Egg said, smiling. "This is so cool, Maddie. Why didn't you tell me sooner? I have a million ideas."

"I know," Madison agreed. "Okay, so for the list of guys, I've got you and Drew, of course—"

"Did someone say my name?" Drew asked from his seat to the left of Egg. He leaned over and smiled at Madison.

"Can we tell him?" Egg asked.

Drew stared at Egg. "Tell me what?"

"Shh!" Madison said. "Okay, we can tell him. But

you guys really can't tell anyone else about this. If word gets around, the surprise will be totally ruined!"

"I won't tell anyone anything," Drew said. "Especially since I have no idea what you're talking about."

"Egg?" Madison asked.

"We promise, we promise," Egg said. Then he turned to Drew. "Big surprise party for Chet this weekend," he explained.

"No way," Drew said. "Awesome!"

"It's for Fiona, too," Madison added.

"Duh, they're twins," Egg said. "So who's invited?"

"That's the question," Madison said. "Any ideas?"

"Dan," Drew said. "We've gotta have Dan there."

"He's on the list," Madison said. "So is Hart. And Suresh." Madison felt her cheeks start to burn at the mention of Hart's name, and she hoped Egg and Drew wouldn't notice.

"That's cool," Egg said. "What about Ben? He and Chet are pretty friendly."

Madison bit her lip, thinking about how Aimee had vetoed Ben on Saturday. "Don't you guys think he's a little . . . obnoxious?" she asked.

Egg shrugged. "Yeah," he said. "So? I'm obnoxious, too."

Drew snorted the way he always did when he laughed at Egg's wisecracks.

"Hey, Chet thinks Ben's hilarious," Drew added.

Madison sighed. "Okay," she said. "He's on the list."

Just then, Mrs. Wing walked over. "I'm sorry, Walter. Samantha's program was a little more complicated than I thought. But I can help you now."

"Oh, it's no problem, Mrs. Wing," Egg said. "Madison and Drew are helping me." Madison had to fight down a giggle. Egg was always extra-polite when he spoke to Mrs. Wing, because he had a little crush on her. It was sort of funny to watch him in action.

Mrs. Wing smiled at them. "Okay, great. Let me go help Ben before the bell rings."

"Don't you need to talk to her?" Madison asked Egg as Mrs. Wing walked away.

"I'll catch her later, during free period," Egg said. "This is more important."

Madison smiled. That was just like the Egg she'd always known—friends always came first with him.

"Add Lance," Drew blurted. "He sits with Chet at lunch sometimes."

"Oh, yeah—he's funny, too," Egg added. "We can get you his e-mail address."

"Great," Madison said just as the bell rang. "Thanks, you guys."

"No problem." Egg stood up to leave.

"Now swear to me one more time that you won't tell anyone about this," Madison said. "No one."

Egg snorted. "I already *did*," he said, walking toward the door. Madison followed him, Drew right behind her.

"I mean it, Egg—you can't tell anyone else," Madison insisted as she stepped into the crowded hall.

"Yeah, yeah," Egg said.

"We won't, Maddie," Drew promised. "It's okay, don't worry."

"Hey, Chet!" Egg called. "Over here!"

Madison froze. Chet was walking right toward her. And Hart was with him! "Oh my gosh!" Madison whispered. "Egg—what are you doing?"

"Would you relax, Maddie?" Egg whispered. "It would look bizarre for me to suddenly stop talking to Chet, right?"

Madison nodded as Chet and Hart walked up to them.

"Hey, guys," Chet said. "What's going on?"

"Hey, Finnster," Hart said, giving Madison a smile. "How are you?"

"Oh, not much," Madison said, and immediately wanted to kick herself. She'd expected Hart to ask her what she was up to, not how she was. "I mean, I'm not feeling like much," she tried to cover, "you know, kind of like a four on a scale from one to ten."

Egg stared at her. "How *does* your mind work?" he teased.

"A four?" Hart said. "That doesn't sound so good. Are you feeling sick or something?" Madison loved the way Hart's voice went up when he asked a question and he got a cute little crease between his eyebrows when he looked concerned. Especially when the person he was concerned about was *her*.

"Maybe I just ate bad chicken tenders in the cafeteria or something," Madison fibbed.

"You'd better get well by Saturday," Egg said.

"Saturday?" Madison repeated. "What about Saturday?"

If Hart hadn't been standing right there, Madison would have socked Egg in the arm. Had she not just made him swear, like, five times that he wouldn't say anything about the party? She shot him the Look of Death.

"Yeah, what's happening Saturday?" Chet asked.

"Oh—nothing," Madison said quickly. "Nothing at all."

Chet looked at her expectantly.

"Well, it's the weekend," Hart started to say.

"And Egg and I are going in-line skating," Madison improvised. "In the park. Wanna come?"

"We are?" Egg asked. Madison elbowed him in the rib. "Oh, right!" he said.

"I love in-line skating," Hart said. "Do you guys mind if I come, too?"

Madison's heart nearly exploded out of her chest. She'd been waiting for a moment like this. So what if the plans were fake?

"Sure!" she cried. "I'll e-mail you where and when." He'd find out about the real Saturday plan later on.

73

"Wait," Hart said. "Let me give you my e-mail address."

Madison reached into her bag for her notebook—but it wasn't there. She, of course, already knew Hart's e-mail address because he had once sent her an e-mail. But she couldn't let him know that she had saved it. And memorized it! "Drag," Madison said with a groan. "I left my notebook back in class."

"Well, don't just stand there," Egg said. "Go get it. I have Hart's e-mail address—I'll let him know what time we're getting together to go in-line skating." He gave Madison a smile, showing her that he was playing along.

"Okay," Madison said, half-trusting Egg to keep his mouth shut about the party. "See you guys later."

She turned and trotted back down the hall, disappointed that she couldn't stay and talk to Hart. But then again, she really *would* see him on Saturday if he came to the party.

"Hello, Madison," Mrs. Wing said as Madison dashed back into the computer lab. She was perched behind her desk, working on her own computer.

"Hi, Mrs. Wing," Madison said, scanning the room. Her orange notebook sat on the desk as if it were patiently awaiting her return.

Mrs. Wing stopped typing. "I'm glad you're here, Madison. I have something for you, but I didn't want to give it to you in front of the other kids."

Madison walked over to Mrs. Wing's large wooden

desk at the front of the room. Its surface was covered with funny little things—a wand full of sparkles, a purple plastic Slinky, and a bendable orange giraffe. Madison's eye fell on a framed picture. A tall man with dark hair and a bright smile was kneeling, his arms wrapped around a wire-haired terrier. Madison knew the man in the photo—Mrs. Wing's husband, Dr. Wing. He was a veterinarian who worked at the Far Hills Animal Clinic, where Madison volunteered.

Mrs. Wing noticed Madison looking at the photo. "Have you been down to the clinic lately?" she asked. "Fleet, one of the collies, just had puppies."

"You're kidding!" Madison said.

"No—you *have* to see them," Mrs. Wing gushed. "They are so cute!"

"I will," Madison promised. She loved Phin, but couldn't resist other dogs, too.

"Here's what I wanted to give to you," Mrs. Wing said, pulling open a desk drawer. Carefully, she picked out a flat plastic box and handed it to Madison. "This is just a little thank-you for all of your hard work on the school Web site. It's a CD-ROM. I know how much you like animals—"

"Animal screen savers!" Madison said as she read the cover. "Oh, thank you, Mrs. Wing! I don't know what to say!" Without even thinking, she leaned over and gave Mrs. Wing a hug. "I can hardly wait to go home and try them out."

Mrs. Wing beamed. "I thought you'd appreciate it."

"I love it!" Madison said. She was luckier than lucky to have Mrs. Wing as her teacher. What teachers gave students gifts? Madison wasn't sure what she wanted to be when she grew up. But she knew she wanted to be like Mrs. Wing.

"You'd better get to class," Mrs. Wing said. "I think the second bell is about to ring."

"I'll hurry," Madison said as she trotted to the door. She paused with her hand on the knob. "And thanks a zillion."

Mrs. Wing waved her hand with a "Shucks, it's nothing" gesture.

"Any time," she said.

And Madison knew she meant it.

"Dinner will be ready in twenty minutes," Mom called upstairs.

Madison was sprawled across her bed, working on her laptop. "Okay!" she said absently as she pulled up her latest file. Outside, rain pattered against her bedroom window. Thundershowers always put Madison in the writing mood.

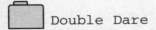 Double Dare

Rude Awakening: To boot or not to boot, that is the question. So far in seventh grade, I've downloaded way more than I can handle.

Did I say download? More like overload.
Fiona's party is only days away, and Aimee
and I haven't even sent out the invitations
yet. And now (stupidly?) I asked for Egg's
help with the guest list. I'm afraid that
he's going to go blabbing about the party
all over town! Why did I ever think that he
could keep his big mouth shut?

At least the Web page Fiona and I are
working on is finally starting to come
together. That is, I think it is. There is
still a lot of work to do—and I need to
add those sound bytes. But when will we
finish it? This weekend is completely shot
because of the party.

We *have* to pull this off. I don't care
if I have to surf every homework page on
the Internet 24/7. Egg made a big mistake
when he dared me to enter the contest.

BIGGER than big.

**Madison closed the file and logged on to bigfish-
bowl.com. When she checked her buddy list, she saw
BalletGrl was online.**

\<MadFinn\>: Hey, you!
\<Balletgrl\>: Hi!!!!!
\<MadFinn\>: Can you believe Fiona's
    party is THIS Saturday?
\<Balletgrl\>: I know--I hear Ben is
    back on the list
\<MadFinn\>: how do u know that? Did Egg
    tell you? I'm going to kill him!!!

\<Balletgrl\>: Um, NM

\<MadFinn\>: Serious! Was it Egg? He is such a (:-D

\<Balletgrl\>: I guess he knew I knew.

\<MadFinn\>: Still. He's supposed to keep his mouth shut

\<Balletgrl\>: You know Egg

\<MadFinn\>: *Sigh* Why am I getting so freaked?

\<Balletgrl\>: Don't worry Maddie :>) if he wants to tell everyone about the party it's NYP

\<MadFinn\>: If he wants to tell everyone about the party it ruins EVERYTHING

\<Balletgrl\>: he won't! He's just excited. And I am, too. We have to finish the invite tho. When can I C U?

\<MadFinn\>: i can do it myself if u want

\<Balletgrl\>: No way! I'll come over after dinner--veggie lasagna, yum

\<MadFinn\>: ick ok gotta go. Mom's calling

\<Balletgrl\>: L8R

\<MadFinn\>: bye

Madison logged off. "Let's go, Phinnie, time for dinner," she told her dog, who was busy sniffing the

backs of her legs. Pugs could be so weird some-times.

But not as weird as some *people* she knew.

What on earth was Egg thinking when he talked to Aimee about the party? Madison wanted to call up Egg that very moment and remind him that he was sworn to secrecy—but decided against it. She'd reminded him so many times already. At this rate, Egg just might start blabbing to get on Madison's nerves.

Even though there was work to be done, Madison was glad Fiona's party was only a few days away. The faster the party date arrived, the less chance Egg would have to blow the surprise!

Chapter 7

"Hi, Mr. Books," Madison said as she pulled a pen out of her backpack. School had just let out, and she had come to the library to finish up some work.

Top-secret work.

"Hello, Madison," Mr. Books replied. He looked at her with mild blue eyes. Madison thought that Mr. Books should have been a secret agent instead of a librarian. It was always so difficult to tell what he was thinking. He passed her the computer log-in notebook like a spy.

"Name and time," he instructed in a low voice. "It's three-thirty on the dot."

Madison scribbled her name on a blank space and started to push the log notebook toward Mr. Books. Her eye spotted another name in the log—Chet Waters? Madison grabbed the notebook back toward her to make sure her eyes weren't playing tricks.

"Is everything all right, Ms. Finn?" Mr. Books asked. He slammed his hand on the log protectively, as though it were something precious that Madison might try to steal.

"Oh, uh, yeah," Madison said, sliding the book back toward him. She glanced around the room. Chet was somewhere in the library. She'd have to be very, very careful about everything she worked on up here.

Madison made her way toward the computers. Chet was nowhere in sight. But that didn't mean anything. He may have just gotten up for a drink of water, or gone to the rest room. Moving quietly past the stacks of reference books, Madison chose a computer in the corner, with a good view of the rest of the library. She wanted to keep her eyes and ears open for Chet.

Even though the school computers were supposed to be used for homework and research only, Madison popped her personal disk into the drive and called up a file she had worked on the night before.

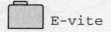 E-vite

Fiona and Chet's Party
TOP-SECRET INVITATION LIST

Aimee	Hart	Ivy
Me	Suresh	Joan
Egg	Ben	Rose
Drew	Daisy	Lance
Lindsay	Dan	

It's funny, when I look at the list of people who are coming to the party, it doesn't seem like such a huge number. But it took two of us days to come up with it—and then we still needed Egg and Drew's help! I thought making a list was going to be the easy part, but it turned out to be the hardest. Designing the layout for the invitation is simple. Figuring out who someone's real friends are is hard.

Rude Awakening: Friendship is like a peanut-butter sandwich. Sometimes it's good, and sometimes it's just plain sticky.

I know that I'll probably regret inviting Ivy and her drones, but there's nothing I can do about it now. Aimee and I sent out the e-vite last night when she came over after dinner. Besides, it's Fiona's party—and I know that Fiona wouldn't want to hurt Ivy's feelings by not inviting her. I think Fiona still likes Ivy . . . although *why* is a mystery to me. She'll learn soon enough about Ivy's true colors.

So what now? All I have left to do is wait for everyone to reply. Who knows? Maybe I'll get lucky and Ivy won't come. LOL. Not too likely. Ivy never misses a party.

Madison opened the JPEG of the invitation she and Aimee had made so she could attach it to her e-vite file. They had run out of time before they could figure out how to put on the sound effects—but the art looked great.

Shhhhh!
LET'S HAVE A BALL @
FIONA AND CHET'S TOP-SECRET
SURPRISE BOWLING PARTY!

Day: Saturday, September 30
Where: Gotta Bowl! Lanes . . . then to
Fiona and Chet's house for cake and presents!
Time: 12:30
(Don't be late, or you could ruin the surprise!)
RSVP to MadFinn@bigfishbowl.com
(Madison Finn)

Madison wondered whether anyone had responded to the invitation yet. She would be checking her e-mail the second she arrived home that afternoon!

"Whooooooa!" Madison yelled. She nearly jumped a foot in the air when someone tapped her right shoulder. And when she looked, there was no one there. That's when she *knew* who it was.

Chet and Egg. Laughing their heads off at her.

"Gotcha, Maddie!" Egg said.

Madison gulped and turned to block the monitor. What was Egg doing, sneaking up on her with Chet? If Chet had seen the party invitation up on her screen, the whole surprise would be ruined! "Ha, ha," Madison smirked. She minimized the JPEG of the e-vite and closed the screen.

"You should've seen your face—priceless!" Egg said, still laughing.

"Yeah, what're you hiding there?" Chet asked, cocking an eyebrow at her screen. "Your Web page?"

"None of your business," Madison said quickly.

"Madison doesn't like to share," Egg said.

"Well, sometimes it's good to keep your mouth shut," Madison snapped, making a face at Egg. "Maybe you ought to practice that, Walter." She used his real name when she wanted to make him squirm.

Egg coughed. "You're *supposed* to talk about things with your friends, Maddie," he said.

"What's THAT supposed to mean?" Madison said.

"Forget it," Egg mumbled. He looked at the floor.

Madison fiddled with a strand of hair. "No—really. Tell me. I want to know."

Egg looked at Chet uncertainly, and Chet looked away.

"Why won't you tell us what you're working on with Fiona?" Egg blurted suddenly. "What's the big secret about your stupid Web page? Are you afraid we'll steal your ideas, or something?"

Madison didn't know how to answer him. He was right. They weren't sharing. They wanted to demolish Egg and Chet—not share. What was that about?

"It's just that—" Madison said, then stopped.

"Just *what*?" Egg asked.

"I don't know," Madison said lamely, even though she did.

"Well it's starting to feel like you don't trust me," Egg said. "We've been friends a long time, Maddie, but maybe it's time for me to log off."

"What?" Madison felt her jaw drop open. Egg wasn't serious, was he? "Thanks a lot," she griped. "You're mad because I won't tell you all about my project, but you didn't even pick me as your partner!"

"What does that have to do with anything?" Egg said.

"It has everything to do with everything!" Madison said loudly.

Mr. Books poked his head around the corner.

"Ms. Finn," Mr. Books said, "I suggest that you and your friends keep your voices down. I like quiet in my library."

"Sorry. But, it doesn't matter," Egg declared. "Because Chet and I were just leaving."

"Very well," Mr. Books said, walking away.

Chet made a face. "That guy acts so strange sometimes."

"He's not the only one!" Egg said, looking directly at Madison. He turned on his heel and strode away. Chet gave Madison a quick, apologetic look and hurried after his friend.

Madison slumped in her chair for a moment, arms crossed. She had come to the media lab to do some work on her Web page, but she had gotten nothing done. And there was no way she could work on it now—her mind was totally overloaded. She closed her files and started packing up to leave. Fresh air would make her feel better.

When Madison stepped into the bright sunshine, her body flooded with warmth and she felt her mood change. Checking her watch, she decided to head over to the soccer fields. Fiona's practice would be finishing up soon. Maybe a talk with her BFF would help her forget about her argument with Egg?

The girls' soccer team was running drills when Madison reached the sidelines. Fiona spotted Madison right away and jogged over.

"Hey, we're almost done," she said breathlessly. "Can you wait a few?"

"Sure," Madison said, dropping her backpack on the soft grass. It was still a little damp from rain the night before.

"Hey, Maddie!" Daisy called from the field. She winked and gave Madison a big thumbs-up. Madison took that to mean that Daisy had read the e-vite.

Madison watched as Fiona and her teammates practiced penalty shots and kicking into the goal. Fiona was really good. The goalie had a hard time keeping up with her powerful kicks.

Before dismissing the team, the coach had everyone huddle up so they could end practice with a quick cheer. Fiona trotted over to Madison.

"Thanks for waiting," she said, picking up her bag from beside the bench.

"No prob," Madison said. She and Fiona fell into step as they walked away from the field.

"I've got some very interesting news," Fiona said, smiling

"What?" Madison asked.

"My dumb brother left his Web page up on the computer last night, and I saw it," Fiona said, waggling her eyebrows.

Madison stopped in her tracks. "You're kidding!"

Fiona shook her head. "No lie. You won't believe this—it's an all-science site, and it's loaded with all these crazy graphics. It even plays this dumb song, which was totally in my head all night." Fiona groaned.

"Sounds really flashy," Madison said, biting her lip.

"Yeah, flashy," Fiona said with a snort. "But it takes forever to load. I think that's why Chet wandered away from the computer—he got sick of waiting for it to pop up."

"Hmmm." Madison pressed her lips together, thinking of her and Fiona's Web page. Sure, it was useful and had a lot of links. It was functional, just as Mrs. Wing and Dad said it should be. But would the judges be more impressed with cool graphics and music? She thought again about adding the sounds . . .

"And now Chet's asked Mom and Dad for

WebScore 3000 for his birthday," Fiona went on. "It's supposed to have amazing graphics for Web-page design. But—whatever—our birthday is on Saturday and the Web pages are due Friday. It's not like he'll really have time to use it—"

A chill skittered down Madison's spine. Fiona had just said the word *birthday* twice. Madison remembered Daisy's wink. Had she let anything slip to Fiona about the party?

"Uh . . . right . . . Saturday," Madison said, trying to sound nonchalant. "Your birthday's this weekend. Are you guys doing anything?"

Fiona sighed. "Just the same old same old, I'm sure," she said. "Mom's barely even mentioned it this year."

"Do you know what you want?" Madison asked, looking at her friend's face carefully. Was Fiona just pretending not to know?

Fiona kicked at a stone on the sidewalk. "I don't know what I want," she said. "I've barely even thought about it. The thing about my birthday, Maddie, is that it isn't ever totally special, because I always have to share it with HIM. Argggh!"

Madison chuckled at the reference to Chet. And she was now satisfied that Fiona had no clue about the party plans.

Either that, or Fiona deserved an Academy Award for this performance.

So the surprise was still on—full steam ahead.

Chapter 8

When Madison got home, she rushed up to her room to boot up her computer and check her e-mail. Had anyone responded to the e-vite? When the screen popped up, she nearly fell off her chair.

FROM	SUBJECT
✉ BalletGrl	Re: Shhh! Top Secret Party!
✉ LuvNstuff	Re: Shhh! Top Secret Party!
✉ W_Wonka7	Re: Shhh! Top Secret Party!
✉ Kickit88	Re: Shhh! Top Secret Party!
✉ Sk8ingboy	Re: Fw: Shhh! Top Secret Party!
✉ Waters	Thank You!
✉ JeffFinn	See You Soon

Madison squealed. There were so many responses so soon—and some were from e-mail addresses that she didn't even recognize!

"But what if . . ." Madison's mind wandered.

"What if these are e-mails saying people *can't* come to the party? Oh, no!"

She quickly selected the first note at the top of the list.

> From: Balletgrl
> To: MadFinn
> Subject: Re: Shhh! Top Secret Party!
> Date: Tues 26 Sept 10:14 AM
>
> Sorry, Maddie, but I'm busy that day. J/K!!! The e-vite looks great--I love the TOP SECRET stuff you added!!!! This is going to be such a blast!!!!
>
> Of course I'm coming . . . I cannot wait for us to make the cake. CU tomorrow. I'll bring the frosting like I said.
>
> Hugs and kisses,
>
> Aim
>
> p.s. I bet ur stressing out about the invites, but DON'T. They look great and I know everyone will come!!!

Madison laughed, feeling slightly less stressed. Aimee was such a good BFF. She knew exactly what

Madison was feeling sometimes before Madison even felt it. Madison moved onto the next e-mail, from Lindsay Frost.

```
From: Luvnstuff
To: MadFinn
Subject: Re: Shhh! Top Secret Party!
Date: Tues 26 Sept 12:22 PM
Hi, Maddie! This looks like so much
fun--I'll definitely be there.

Thanks so much for inviting me!
Lindsay
```

The next two e-mails were both acceptances, too. Drew said he couldn't wait until Saturday and Daisy asked what she should wear. Madison breathed a sigh of relief. Not only did it look like this party was really going to happen, but people were sounding genuinely excited about it.

Madison had to catch her breath when she opened the next e-mail reply.

```
From: Sk8ing Boy
To: MadFinn
Subject: Re: Fw: Shhh! Top Secret
Party!
Date: Tues 26 Sept 1:16 PM
Hey, Finnster! Egg told me no
blading on Sat. I guess THIS is why.
```

You are totally gonna surprise
them. I'll be there 4 sure.
Coolness!

I really like the invitation, BTW.

Hart

Madison reread Hart's e-mail five more times. He
didn't just *like* the invitation—he *really liked* it.
Madison hit SAVE and moved the e-mail into its own
special file: HJ.

Even better than getting the e-mail from Hart,
however, was NOT getting one from Ivy or her
drones. Did this mean that they hadn't gotten the e-
vite? Or were they NOT coming? Madison could only
cross her fingers and toes. She'd have to be patient
and read on.

From: Waters
To: MadFinn; Balletgrl
Subject: Thank You!
Date: Tues 26 Sept 2:01 PM
Aimee and Madison,
I am so impressed with all the work
you girls have done. This invitation
looks wonderful! Mr. Waters
said he'd never seen such a nice
invitation. Thank you both so much
for all of your help.

I do need your help with one
more thing. If it isn't too much
trouble, would you girls let me
know what kinds of food and sodas
you think people would like to have
at the party? It's coming up so
soon!

Helen Waters

Food? Sodas? Madison couldn't believe how
much work it was to plan a party. She shot off a
quick response to Mrs. Waters, copying Aimee on
the reply.

From: MadFinn
To: Waters; Balletgrl
Subject: Re: Thank you!
Date: Tues 26 Sept 3:44 PM
Hi, Mrs. Waters!
Lots of people have already
responded to the e-vite. Isn't that
great? Thanks for saying all those
nice things. It was no problem!
I'll send you a list of everyone's
names as soon as I hear from them.

I know you were going to do it,
but Aimee and I want to bake the
birthday cake. Is that all right

with you? I think Fiona likes
chocolate. Does Chet?

We'll think about what other food
would be fun, too, like you asked.
I think people will be happy with
pizza and any kind of juice. I like
root beer.

Please write back.

Maddie

**Madison clicked SEND, and watched as the
message disappeared into cyberspace. She knew the
next message was from Dad.**

From: JeffFinn
To: MadFinn
Subject: See You
Date: Tues 26 Sept 4:01 PM
Dinner still on? I'll pick you up
out front of the house around 7:30.
Stephanie is meeting us @ the
restaurant @ 8. Indian food ok?
Hope so!

Love, Dad

Madison got up from her desk and flopped onto

her bed. She had four hours more to chill out before Dad got there—and she felt so relaxed now!

"I guess I didn't really realize how worried I was about this party," Madison said to Phinnie, who was asleep by her feet, as usual. "But it really looks as though everything is coming together . . ."

"Honey bear?" Mom asked, poking her head through the door. "Are you talking to someone?"

"Hi, Mom," Madison said. "Just talking to myself."

Phin waddled over to Mom to say hello and then sat by the side of Madison's bed until she leaned over and picked him up.

"How's the party planning?" Mom asked.

"Excellent," Madison replied. "Almost everyone is coming! Now all we have to do is bake the cake, if Mrs. Waters says that's okay. She asked if we'd help make a list of other food and drinks kids would like, too. There is so much to do when you plan a party."

"Hmm." Mom tugged on a piece of hair—one of her classic thinking gestures. "Well, I have an idea. Since it's a party for twins, maybe you could serve food that comes in pairs. Like, give everyone two scoops of ice cream?"

Madison giggled. "Yeah—on those side-by-side cones," she said. "What else comes in twos?"

"Twinkies!" Mom said.

Madison chimed in. "And Yodels and Ring Dings and—"

"Stop!" Mom said. "Whatever happened to carrot sticks?"

"They don't come in twos, Mom," Madison said.

Mom laughed. "I think you're doing a super job."

"I hope this party is going to be greater than great," Madison cried. "Right, Phinnie?"

Phin rolled over so Madison would scratch his belly.

For the first time in days, Madison felt as though the surprise party and almost everything else was under control.

Almost.

"Hi, Dad," Madison said, rushing down to the driveway to meet Dad's car. It was 7:46—not 7:30 as he'd said. He was late, as usual.

"Hello, Maddie!" Dad said when she approached the car. He leaned over to give her a kiss. "Nice top. Is it new?"

"This old thing?" Madison said, smiling as she buckled her seat belt. Dad was good at giving just the right compliments. "Where are we eating?"

"Bombay Palace," Dad said. "You like that place, right?"

"Sure, as long as I can get that tandooey skewer thing," Madison said.

"Tandoori chicken?" Dad said, chuckling.

"You bet," Madison said. Bombay Palace was one of her favorite restaurants. Even more than the food, Madison loved the atmosphere. They played music from Indian movies, and the interior was decorated with strings of teeny white Christmas lights. But best of all, Bombay Palace had the ultimate location.

"We go by Far Hills Animal Clinic on the way, right?" Madison asked. "Dad, could we stop there for just a second? Mrs. Wing said that one of the collies just had puppies, and I really want to see them."

Dad checked the clock on the dashboard. "Well . . ." he hedged. "We've got a reservation, and I don't want to keep Stephanie waiting."

"Oh," Madison said, deflated like a balloon losing air. Even though Madison didn't love the idea that Dad was dating, Stephanie was always nice, she had to admit that. Madison could understand why Dad didn't want her to be sitting by herself in the restaurant.

But, she still wanted to make the detour to see the puppies.

"I swear I will only go in for a split second," Madison pleaded.

"I know you," Dad said, "You'll see one puppy and hold it. And then you'll want to hold all of them. . . . Maybe we can go there after dinner?"

"They'll be closed then," Madison said. "Please, Dad? Puh-leeez?"

"Okay," Dad sighed. "Okay. But you'll have to be quick."

"I will, cross my heart," Madison said, giving him a peck on the cheek.

Dad pulled into the parking lot of the Far Hills Animal Clinic, and Madison opened the car door and jumped right out. "Five minutes only," she said. "I know."

"What about me?" Dad replied, "I want to see the puppies, too."

"You do?" Madison said. She grinned as Dad scrambled out of the car and they walked into the clinic.

"Maddie!" said a blonde woman behind the desk. It was Eileen Ginsburg, animal nurse at the clinic and the mother of Madison's friend from school, Dan.

"You're here to see Fleet's pups, aren't you?" Eileen said.

Madison nodded and introduced Dad. After the grown-ups said their polite hellos, Eileen showed them into the back room. A volunteer was there tending to a sick kitten. Dan was there, too, washing cages.

"Hey, Maddie!" Dan yelled. He volunteered at the clinic after school to help his mom out. Madison admired how good he was with the animals. "Did you hear that Fleet had puppies?"

"Yes!" Madison said. "That's why I'm here. Your mom guessed right away." Madison introduced Dad.

"You've got your hands full here," Dad said.

"Yes sir," Dan said. "Let's go see the dogs. There are seven. Can you believe it?"

Dan led them to a low basket lined with blankets in the corner of the room. "We thought she needed some extra space," Dan explained. "Usually we don't have special setups like this, but sometimes. Fleet is special."

Fleet lay on her side, looking exhausted, while seven tiny collie puppies nursed at her side. Madison sucked in her breath. The puppies were so little that they hadn't even opened their eyes yet! "They're adorable," she gasped.

"They really are," Dad agreed, sneaking up behind Madison. "Lucky dogs."

"Dad!" Madison groaned.

"They're only four days old," Dan said. "You can't touch them yet, or else I'd let you hold one."

"Oh, that's okay," Madison said. "I'm happy just to look." She gazed at the puppies again, until she noticed Dad checking his watch. "Whoops! Hey, Dan, we have to boogie."

"So soon?" he said.

"Yeah," Madison said, smiling at Dad. "But thanks so much for showing them to us."

"It was nice to meet you, young man," Dad said.

"Come back and see them again," Dan said. "They get cuter every day."

"I don't see how they could get any cuter," Madison said, "but I'll definitely come back."

Dan showed them out. "Oh, by the way, Maddie, I got your e-mail invitation. It sounds like fun."

"So you'll be there?" Madison said. "So many people are coming. I can't wait." She waved to Dan as she walked to Dad's car.

Madison drifted in a happy-puppy fog all the way to the restaurant. When they arrived, Stephanie was sitting at a table, looking at a menu.

"Sorry we're a little late," Dad said as he leaned over to say hello. "We had to stop and see some puppies."

"Puppies? Wow! Where did you see those?" Stephanie said. She looked at Madison. "I bet that was your idea."

Madison smiled. "Yeah, well this collie had puppies at the animal clinic downtown. I begged Dad to go. Sorry it made us late."

"Nonsense!" Stephanie said. "I remember when my dog Max had puppies on the ranch and we watched them be born."

"Really?" Madison said. Stephanie had the best stories from growing up.

The waiter came over with menus and took the drink orders. Dad requested an appetizer of vegetable samosas. Madison had never tried those before. He always made her try one new thing every time they ate out.

"So how's school, Maddie?" Dad asked, changing the subject.

"Oh—the usual," Madison said.

"Madison has entered a Web-page contest," Dad told Stephanie. "And I think she can win."

Madison rolled her eyes. "Dad . . ." she moaned.

"What? I'm not allowed to be proud of my daughter?" Dad asked. "How's it coming, by the way?"

"Actually, it's going pretty well," Madison admitted. "Fiona and I have been following your advice, keeping it simple. The link you sent to us really helped. It's hard work, though."

"Sounds like it," Stephanie said. "And what else is going on? Any exciting dances or parties coming up?"

"Actually, my friend Aimee and I have been planning a surprise party for our other friends Fiona and Chet. They're twins," Madison explained. "We're going bowling."

"Twins?" Stephanie exclaimed. "My goodness. Twice as much fun then!"

"Who's coming?" Dad asked. "The usual suspects?"

"Yeah," Madison said—then stopped. "Actually, I *think* everyone is coming. I'm not sure about Egg, but everyone else says they'll be there."

Dad's eyebrows shot up. "What's up with Egg?" he asked.

Madison looked down at the pink tablecloth. "Well, he hasn't RSVP'd," Madison admitted. "He and I sort of had a fight."

"A fight?" Dad repeated. "What about?"

Madison glanced up at Stephanie. For some reason, she didn't want to talk about this in front of Dad's girlfriend. "It's nothing, Dad," Madison said quickly. "Can we drop it?"

"But you and Egg are best friends," Dad pressed. "Tell me what's going on. I don't like to hear that you're not speaking . . ."

"Jeff—" Stephanie said.

"Wait, I want to hear this. Tell me why you're not talking, Maddie."

"Dad, didn't you hear me? I said, forget it, okay?" she snapped. The last thing she wanted right now was to relive the whole Egg ordeal.

"Madison, you can talk to me about anything, you know—" Dad said.

"Jeff—" Stephanie tried to interrupt him again.

"It's no biggie, all right? Egg is just being a wiener, as usual."

"A what?" Dad said. "What did you say?" He glanced over at Stephanie, and she put her hand on his arm. "Madison, I don't like it when—"

"Why don't you just listen? I don't want to talk about it!" Madison said.

"Jeff—" Stephanie tried to intervene again.

"Just leave me alone, Dad!" Madison shouted. "Go on another business trip or something, why don't you?"

Dad sat back in his chair, stunned. Madison hardly ever raised her voice at him. She never did it in public. Why was she doing it now? She gulped down her glass of ice water and stared at the wall. Why had those words slipped out?

Madison just wanted to run away.

"I was only trying to help," Dad said softly. Madison could tell by his voice that she'd hurt his feelings, but she didn't know what to say. She couldn't believe she'd said that stuff about a business trip.

"Jeff," Stephanie said, "I think maybe we should change the subject. Let Madison just sit quietly, okay?"

Dad bristled at Stephanie. "Please, don't tell me what to do with my daughter, Steph," he said, his voice strained. Madison couldn't believe that Stephanie was coming to her defense and that Dad was reacting the way he was. It felt like the way things were with Dad and Mom before the Big D.

The waiter came over with the drinks and appetizers. But when Dad handed Madison her vegetable samosa, she pushed it away. She couldn't eat. She couldn't look at him, either. No one was talking now.

Dinner took forever. The ride home was long and hot. Dad and Stephanie spoke in the front seat about work, trying to include Madison in the conversation. But she didn't feel like talking to anyone. She wanted everything just to stop or start over, or something other than this. She needed to be back home with Phin.

Madison thought she'd been on top of the world, planning the party and Web page. So why had she snapped at Dad? Would he ever forgive her for starting the fight in the restaurant?

Gramma Helen told Madison once that there were moments in life when everything crashed in at once, like a big wave. And at those moments, sometimes you felt lost. There, in the backseat of Dad's car, a place that had always been supersafe, Madison felt lost.

Didn't Dad remember what it was like to be in seventh grade?

After a quick good night to Dad and Stephanie, Madison ran inside to say an even quicker hello to Mom and then headed directly upstairs. Phin panted all the way up the stairs behind her.

Luckily, there was one person who *could* understand what she was feeling right now. And that someone could give her good advice, too.

"Hello, laptop," Madison said, logging on to her computer. "I'm back."

```
From: MadFinn
To: Bigwheels
Subject: HELP
Date: Tues 26 Sept 9:00 PM
```
I need ur help big time. I'm having friend and parent angst. I just got into the hugest fight with my Dad.

And I had a fight earlier today
with my friend Egg. I feel like I
am fighting with everyone.
Meanwhile, I'm trying to plan this
party and do work for that contest.
My head is exploding!

Please meet me in a chat room or
e-mail me back ASAP?

Yours till the tree tops,

Maddie

Chapter 9

Apologies

Remember that crashing wave that Gramma Helen talked about? Well, now here comes a mega monster wave. It's Wipeout City.

Fiona thinks that we're being too mean to Egg. Scratch that. She thinks *I'm* being too mean to Egg. I guess Chet (that fat mouth!) told her all about my Egg argument in the library the other day, and now she thinks that I'm only interested in the contest so that I can show Egg up. She's acting a little cold to me, I think. Great. The party is in two days and Fiona is mad.

NO ONE—and I mean absolutely NO ONE—gets where I'm coming from these days.

I mean, I'll admit that part of what Fiona says is true. Showing up Egg *is* part of the reason that I'm in the contest. But it isn't the only reason. The fact is that our Web page is looking greater than great. It has a bunch of different sections: English, Math, Social Studies, History, Science and Technology, Art and Music, and even Foreign Languages. Each section has a different graphical theme, and links to the most helpful sites we could find. We have a real shot at winning this thing.

So Fiona is pressuring me to apologize to Egg, but I just don't want to. I know that she's seriously crushing on him—but I can't get around my feelings. I really wanted to be on Egg's team and he blew me off. And he's the one who turned it into this double dare. I won't apologize.

And it's the same thing with Dad. I can't believe I yelled at him last night—I *never* do stuff like that. But I felt like he just didn't get what I was saying, and it was frustrating. Even though he was *trying*, it didn't really help. And now he's off on one of his business trips, and I can't even call him to apologize. See?

Rude Awakening: If there are two sides to every situation, why am I always on the *wrong* side?

Madison heard the doorbell ring and quickly hit SAVE. She leaped up from the desk and ran downstairs.

107

She knew who was at the door. This person could surely snap her out of the little blue funk, right?

"Presenting . . . the missing ingredients!" Aimee said, twirling around with a big brown paper bag. She'd fixed her blond hair in a loose topknot and her cheeks were pink. "Sorry I'm late. Ballet class ran over."

"Thank goodness you're here!" Madison said, and opened the door wide so Aimee could twirl inside.

"I am so ready to bake," Aimee declared. "And I brought chocolate frosting and a bunch of other stuff we can use to decorate the cake. Roger was a big help, actually." Roger was Aimee's oldest brother, and he knew how to do almost everything—including cook.

"Great!" Madison said with a smile. "This is going to be so much fun!" She could feel the blue funk fading already.

Mom was pouring herself a glass of cranberry juice when Madison and Aimee walked into the kitchen. "Hi, Aimee," Mom said. "Are you girls all set to bake Fiona's cake now?"

"Yep," Aimee said, dropping her bag on the counter.

"Need any help?" Mom asked, taking a sip from her glass.

"Nope," Aimee said.

Mom smiled. "Well, you don't mind if I supervise

the oven part of this afternoon, do you? You need to be careful."

"Of course, Mom," Madison said, giving Aimee the eye. "Where did we put Gramma Helen's recipe card for Super Fudge cake?"

Mom rifled through the cards inside an old wooden recipe box that she hardly ever used. She pulled out an old, stained card and handed it to Madison. "There you go. All the ingredients should be in the cabinets and the fridge. And I bought more flour yesterday."

"What did Mrs. Waters decide about the rest of the food for the party?" Aimee asked.

"Pizza—all the way," Madison said. "And some ice cream for dessert with the cake."

"Man, this will really blow my diet!" Aimee said.

"You're on a diet?" Mom asked.

Aimee shrugged. "Well, sort of."

"Hey, Aimee, Mom says we should serve everything in twos since it's a birthday party for both Chet and Fiona. Isn't that a cool idea? Unfortunately, we couldn't really come up with food that's served in pairs."

"That is brilliant!" Aimee exclaimed. She balanced on the tips of her shoes as though she was doing a ballet move. "Totally, positively, absolutely BRILLIANT!"

"What are you talking about?" Madison asked.

"Let's make *two* cakes," Aimee explained, "*Twin* cakes, get it?"

Madison threw her hands into the air and

hugged her friend. "Aimee, you're a genius! Why didn't I think of that?"

"But you *did* think of it, silly," Aimee replied. "I just helped you."

"Let me just make sure we have enough to make two cakes," Mom said as she pulled the eggs out of the refrigerator. Quickly, Madison and Aimee loaded up the countertop with the rest of the ingredients. They were almost out of baking powder, but when Mom measured it, it turned out that there was enough.

"Bummer. We'll need more frosting," Aimee said. "I only brought enough for one cake. Let me call my dad, or Roger. They can stop at the store on the way home from the bookstore."

"Sounds good," Mom said. "Why don't I let you girls get cooking? Call me if you need anything." She disappeared into her office.

Aimee and Madison sifted and stirred everything together for about an hour. It took so long because they couldn't help but gossip in between.

Phin helped too, snatching up every scrap that found its way to the floor. When Madison pulled the chocolate-covered beaters from the batter and carried them to the sink, Phin followed her so intently that he didn't see Aimee walking toward the cabinet with the bag of flour. She tripped over him and the sack of flour went flying—all over Phinnie! Even a good shake didn't get all of the white powder off him. And he couldn't stop snorting.

"Mom!" Madison called out, laughing. Aimee rushed around with a wet dish towel trying to get the flour picked up, but she only made things worse. The white powder turned into white, wet lumps.

Mom raced into the kitchen. "Oh, my!" she said. "Aimee, stop that! We can sweep it up, don't use a wet rag."

Aimee dropped the towel, which fell on top of Phin with a plop.

"Rowroooooooeeeeeee!" he wailed.

"Oh, Phinnie," Mom said. "I'm afraid you'll need a bath now." She whisked him away, half-laughing at the mess. "And while I'm gone, you girls need to clean up, okay?"

Phin looked at Aimee and Madison from over Mom's shoulder. He licked his lips but scowled when he realized the white stuff on his face didn't taste so great. Madison and Aimee burst into a fit of giggles.

After Mom left the room, they put finishing touches on the first gooey chocolate-on-chocolate cake. Someone tapped at the kitchen sliding door. They turned around to see Aimee's mom standing there with Blossom, the Gillespie family dog. Mrs. Gillespie held Blossom on a leash with one hand and toted a plastic bag in the other.

"Frosting, anyone?" On the other side of the glass, Mrs. Gillespie dangled the bag. "I heard that you needed more ingredients."

"Mommy, hello!" Aimee cried.

"Hi, Mrs. Gillespie!" Madison said as she pulled open the door.

Aimee's basset hound, Blossom, bounded inside. Madison stooped to pet the dog's soft ears.

"Don't worry, Blossom," Madison said. "Phin is just getting a bath. He'll be back in here any minute." Blossom wagged her tail as though she understood. She really was Phin's girlfriend.

"This cake looks great," Mrs. Gillespie said. "Dad told me you're making twin cakes. Who's this one for?"

"I guess this one can be for Fiona," Aimee said, digging a small tube of white frosting out of the bag. "Madison, do you want to do the writing?"

"Your handwriting is better than mine," Madison said. "Go ahead."

Aimee jumped at the chance. She used her best script to write out Happy Birthday, Fiona, and stepped back from the cake proudly.

"What is that supposed to be?" Madison asked.

"What do you mean?" Aimee said, licking a little frosting off her pinky.

"It says 'Happy Birthday, Fion,' " Madison said.

"It does? Oh my God! I ran out of room! Maddie, I didn't even—" Aimee pulled at her hair. "I am so sorry. I ruined it."

"Aimee, calm down," Mrs. Gillespie said. "It's only frosting."

Mom came down the stairs to see what the commotion was all about. She'd given Phin a sponge bath instead of a full dunking.

"Melanie!" Mom said, greeting Mrs. Gillespie. "So they got you in on the cake baking, too, I see."

"Look!" Madison said. "I solved the problem. We can squish in the missing 'A' and it looks fine."

Phin wriggled out of Mom's arms and ran happy circles around Blossom. Blossom, who was about three times Phin's size, expressed her joy at seeing him by lying down in the middle of the kitchen and yawning. Everyone stopped to laugh at the odd couple.

Mom offered Mrs. Gillespie some tea while Madison pulled the second cake out of the oven.

"We need to wait for this to cool down before we frost it," Madison explained. "Is it okay if Aimee and I go up to my room for a little while?"

"Sure, we'll hold down the fort . . . er, kitchen," Mom said.

"Take your time," Mrs. Gillespie agreed, blowing on her tea.

"Let's see if anyone else has replied to the e-vite," Aimee said as she followed Madison upstairs.

"Great idea." Madison logged onto bigfishbowl.com and checked her e-mail account. There were two new e-mails in her in box.

```
FROM     SUBJECT
✉ L8RG8R   Re: Fw: Shhh! Top Secret Party!
✉ Flowr99  Re: Fw: Shhh! Top Secret Party!
```

"Who's that?" Aimee asked, twirling a piece of hair around her index finger.

"Not sure," Madison said. "These are some of the people Egg forwarded the invite to."

```
From: L8RG8R
To: MadFinn
Subject: Re: Fw: Shhh! Top Secret
   Party!
Date: Thurs 28 Sept 1:14 PM
Hey, I'm definitely coming to Chet's
party. Thanks for inviting me!

Lance
```

"Lance is that guy who always acts like a dork?" Aimee asked. She could be hypercritical of boys sometimes, Madison noticed. But all the boys liked Aimee, no matter what she said.

"Lance is really okay," Madison said, defending him.

"I'll bet the other e-mail is from Rose," Aimee said, eyeing the screen name Flowr99. "Open it."

The note was not from a drone, however.

It came from the Queen Bee herself.

From: Flowr99
To: MadFinn
Subject: Re: Fw: Shhh! Top Secret
   Party!
Date: Thurs 28 Sept 2:34 PM
Nice invitation, Madison. I didn't
know you knew how to use a JPEG.

Of course I'm coming to the party--I
know it won't be any fun for you
without your seventh-grade Class
President. Besides, someone has to
be there to make sure Fiona has a
good time. TTFN!

Ivy

"Ivy!" Madison and Aimee exclaimed.

"So it's really true," Aimee said with a groan. "She's actually coming."

"I'll bet that means that Phony Joanie and Rose Thorn are coming, too, even if they haven't bothered to RSVP," Madison said. Scanning Ivy's message again, she added, "Maybe this wasn't such a good idea."

"Maybe?" Aimee repeated, wide eyed. "Don't look at me—I tried to warn you. Remember what she did at your third-grade birthday party?"

Madison shook her head. "Please don't remind me—"

"I gave you that poster book," Aimee prompted, "and she grabbed it and totally hogged it."

"Oh, right!" Madison said, remembering. "She was kissing that singer's photo all night. She kept saying that he was her boyfriend and wouldn't let anyone else look at it. I remember!"

"Why were we ever friends with her?" Aimee asked, staring at the ceiling.

"I have no idea," Madison said.

But she did remember. Ivy had been different then. Back in third grade, Ivy's obnoxiousness had been more of a streak, and less of a stain. Back then, Ivy hadn't needed to be the star of everything.

"I can't believe she's actually coming," Aimee went on. "And there's no way we can get out of it now . . . the party is only two days away!"

"I know," Madison agreed, shaking her head. The week had flown by quicker than quick—and now everything was here. The deadline for her Web page was tomorrow!

Madison and Aimee went back downstairs and finished up the second cake. Then Aimee, Blossom, and Mrs. Gillespie said their good-byes. Mom decided to make grilled cheese sandwiches and soup for dinner. Madison went back up to her room and tested out the links for her Web page after they ate.

"Are you getting ready for bed, honey bear?" Mom asked from the hallway.

"In a few minutes," Madison promised. "I'm just finishing this up."

"Okay. Don't stay up too late," Mom said. "You have a big weekend coming up."

"I won't," Madison promised. Phin came in and curled up at her feet.

When she was finally satisfied that all of her HTML codes were working, Madison logged into bigfishbowl once more and typed a quick e-mail to her Web-page partner, Fiona.

```
From: MadFinn
To: Wetwinz
Subject: We Did It!
Date: Thurs 28 Sept 10:27 PM
```
Hey, U--just wanted to say good luck tomorrow! (To both of us!) :o)

I think the page looks great. UR a great partner!!!!!

Good night, sleep tight . . . DLTBBB!!!!

xoxoxo

Maddie

Madison logged off and went to the bathroom to brush her teeth. Then she turned out the lights

117

and crawled under her comforter. Today had been a baking success. And she hadn't really thought of Egg, or Dad, or even Ivy all day.

But lying there in the dark, familiar thoughts and worries churned through her brain. She could deny it all she wanted, but Madison needed to apologize.

But when?

Through her window, Madison watched the round, white moon. Below it was a bright star. Pulling her comforter up to her chin the way she used to when she was a little girl, she closed her eyes.

And Madison made a wish that everything would turn out all right.

Chapter 10

"Are you ready?" Madison asked Fiona as she slid into a chair beside her friend.

"Are you kidding?" Fiona replied. "This Web page contest is *ours*." She flashed Madison a confident smile, and Madison smiled back.

"All right, everyone," Mrs. Wing said. "Let's see your Web pages. Anyone who still needs my help, this is your last chance."

A chorus of "Mrs. Wing!"s went up, and at least ten hands shot into the air. Madison typed her and Fiona's Web address into the computer, and the Web page appeared on the screen.

In front of Madison, Egg and Chet were laughing their heads off at something. Madison tried to ignore them—until Fiona leaned over and whispered in her ear, "There he is."

Madison scowled at the computer monitor. "I know," she said.

"So, go tell him you're sorry," Fiona urged. "You said you were looking for the right time to do it. . . ."

Madison knew that her friend had a point, but she didn't want to tell Egg she was sorry in front of Chet and everyone else in their computer class.

Egg pointed to something on the screen in front of him, and Chet started laughing so hard that his shoulders were shaking.

Madison looked over. "What's so funny?" she asked in her friendliest voice.

"Fiona's face!" Chet howled. Egg laughed even louder.

Madison stood there with her arms crossed until the boys stopped laughing. Egg turned and looked at Madison coldly.

"Just our Web page," he said.

"Um . . . Can I see it?" Madison asked, trying to be nicer again.

Egg shrugged. "Whatever."

The boys' page was up on their screen, and Madison scanned the images and text. At the top was a picture of two Jedi warriors from the latest Star Wars movie—only Chet and Egg had put their own heads on top of the bodies. Their light sabers clashed every couple of seconds, letting out an electronic *pzzzap* sound. Chet scrolled down the page to reveal a message:

A short, short time ago
in a galaxy not too far from here
lived two heroes who struggled with
homework so boring that it put them to sleep.
Our heroes decided that there had to be a better way.
And so they created the Science Stunner—a Web page
packed with cool science and games
for when they needed a break.
Now they could work for hours—or at least make their
parents *think* they were working.
This is their Web site. . . .

Music bleated from the computer speakers as Chet continued to scroll down. The two had packed the page with links to many different science and gaming sites. They even had little video clips of themselves, dressed as Jedi knights, giving reviews of each site. Madison pressed her lips together. She had to admit it—Chet and Egg's page looked *great*. The page she and Fiona had been working on, which had looked so cute with its simple graphics and fun, rhyming text, was boring by comparison.

Way boring.

Mrs. Wing appeared at Egg's elbow. "How's it coming along, boys?"

"It's coming along very well, Mrs. Wing," Egg said, blushing a little.

"Take a look," Chet said.

"Hmmmm," Mrs. Wing peered at the Web page. "You boys really put a lot of effort into this."

Chet and Egg grinned at each other. "Yessssss!" they both said at the same time.

Mrs. Wing took the mouse and clicked on one of their links. She waited a moment, but nothing happened. "Hmm . . ." she said, clicking the link again.

Madison tried not to smile, even though she was secretly happy about Chet and Egg's misfortune.

Mrs. Wing hit the REFRESH button.

"I think the computer is frozen," she said. "I'm not getting anything. Try refreshing the page a few times more, please. Otherwise, you guys had better reboot. We don't want our classroom systems crashing."

Egg frowned. "This always happens," he moaned.

"Well," Mrs. Wing said, "sometimes that happens when you're dealing with a lot of graphics. A few other people are having that problem."

Madison gulped. Other people were having that problem? Did that mean that everyone else in the class had used more graphics than she and Fiona had? Would their links work?

"I'll come back around to see you boys once you get that page up again," Mrs. Wing promised. She moved along to Madison and Fiona's station.

Madison felt her heart start to beat. What would Mrs. Wing think of their site—especially now that she'd seen Egg and Chet's superdeluxe page?

"Let's see what you girls have done," Mrs. Wing

said. Her bracelets rattled against the keyboard as she viewed the page. Madison held her breath as Mrs. Wing punched a few of the links. Thankfully, they had each tested them all the night before.

Mrs. Wing stood up. "Class, may I have your attention? Everyone, please come here for a minute."

"Is everything okay?" Madison asked, suddenly worried that her favorite teacher was going to point out everything that was wrong with their page in front of the entire class. She suspected the worst.

"Yes," Mrs. Wing said. "You and Fiona have done a wonderful job. This is a really useful page. I would like everyone in the class to see it."

Fiona turned to Madison and squeezed her forearm. "Did you hear that?" she said softly. Madison sat up straight in her chair, smiling, while Mrs. Wing pointed out the finer points of MADISON AND FIONA'S HOMEWORK CENTER.

Mrs. Wing said their page followed the rules exactly and was just the kind of practical site the contest judges would be expecting. Madison made a silent mental note to thank Dad for his help. He'd been right all along.

"Now, class, I want everyone to download and print your pages. I want to put them on display on the bulletin board." Mrs. Wing pointed to a blank board at the back of the room. Madison hadn't noticed it when she walked in, but now she saw that at the top was a large banner that read: HOW A WEB PAGE IS MADE.

Fiona and Madison couldn't stop grinning, which must have annoyed Chet and Egg. They stood across the room, moping. Their Web page screen froze again right after they rebooted the computer.

Madison glanced over, hoping to catch Egg's eye. He looked straight at her as she mouthed the word.

"Sorry," Madison said silently.

Unfortunately, Egg didn't take that as an apology. He thought Madison was rubbing it in.

"Hey, Maddie," Aimee said, leaning against the locker next to Madison's. The last bell had just rung and they were out for the weekend, but Aimee could tell that Madison wasn't in a great mood. "What's wrong? Fail locker inspection again?"

"Ha-ha," Madison said as two spiral-bound notebooks fell from her locker, a pile of papers fluttering after them.

Madison shoved everything back into her own messy locker and slammed it closed.

"Seriously," Aimee pressed, "you're looking a little down."

"I know. I had this terrible fight with Egg . . . and I feel like even though Fiona and I got some compliments on our Web page, we could have done a better job," Madison admitted.

"Egg, shmeg . . . your page was the best." Aimee

gave Madison a little poke in the shoulder. "You should be happy!" She did a little twirl. "Besides, the You Know What for You Know Who is this weekend—and we're going to the You Know Where, which will be a blast!"

Madison laughed. Aimee was practically leaping down the hall. Once again, her BFF cheered her up. It was too late to worry about the contest. Madison needed to be thinking about the party instead.

"Hey, wait up!" Fiona shouted behind them. Madison and Aimee stopped to wait for their friend. "You are the best, partner!" Fiona said happily to Madison as she jogged up. "I think we have a chance of winning the contest, don't you?"

"Your teacher saw the Web page?" Aimee asked.

"Mrs. Wing totally loved it," Fiona explained. "She made everyone in the whole class look at it!"

Aimee stared at Madison. "That is so excellent. So why are you moping around like a sourpuss?"

"I just said that I thought it could be better. . . ." Madison said lamely.

Aimee blew her bangs out of her eyes with an impatient burst of air. "Okay, no more talking about this. You definitely don't get any sympathy from me now that I know everyone loved it."

Madison grinned sheepishly. "Okay," she said. "You're right."

"So, Fiona," Aimee said slyly as she pushed open the heavy school doors, "want to get together tomorrow? We could go to Freeze Palace or some-thing for your birthday."

Outside, the late September sun was warm on Madison's face, and she smiled up at it. Aimee was trying secretly to get Madison's head in a different place. If she thought about the birthday party, she wouldn't think about the Web page anymore.

"Sorry, I can't really do anything on Saturday," Fiona said. "My dad is taking us to see these old col-lege friends of his—we'll be gone all day."

"He *what*?" Madison asked, as if she didn't understand English. She gaped at Aimee, who was staring at Fiona, openmouthed.

"Your—your dad?" Aimee stammered.

"Yeah," Fiona said, rolling her eyes. "Since we moved, our aunt and uncle can't come over this year. So he's taking us to see these old friends of his. They have kids our age, and I guess we met them once about five hundred years ago and had a good time playing in the sandbox, or whatever. I don't even remember them, but Dad's all excited about it, even though Chet and I both said we'd rather stay here."

"Does your mom know about this?" Madison asked.

"Of course," Fiona said. "But it was just a last-minute thing—that's why I didn't tell you about it before."

"Wow," Aimee said hoarsely, "that's—that's great." Madison could tell by her voice that Aimee thought the plan was anything but great. What about the surprise? Had Mrs. Waters forgotten? It didn't make sense.

"But we can get together on Sunday," Fiona said. "If that's okay. I do want to do *something* fun for my birthday."

Madison bit back a groan. *Sunday*? She wondered briefly whether she would now have to call all the guests and tell them to come the next day. There was no way everyone would be able to make a new date on such short notice. What a mess! Not even Aimee could cheer her up after this. Fiona's dad had really thrown a King Kong–size wrench into things. After all the work they'd done, now Madison and Aimee were going to be sitting at a bowling alley with a ton of guests, twin chocolate cakes—and no guests of honor!

Madison could already hear what Poison Ivy Daly would have to say about that.

 Party Time

I can't believe it—the day of the party is finally HERE!!

Yesterday, I thought Fiona's surprise party was toast, as in *flambé*. So I sent Fiona's mom a way frantic e-mail, asking her whether we should tell everyone that the plans were off. But it turns out that Mrs. Waters was just being a supersneak! She and Mr. Waters totally handed Fiona and Chet this fake story about going to visit these college friends of his. The only place they're going is for a long drive around Far Hills . . . and then to the bowling alley! It's perfect, because this way, Mrs. Waters, Aimee, and I will have plenty of time to set up.

I have to admit, Mrs. Waters has a way with the surprise party . . . she even fooled Aimee and me!

I can't wait I can't wait I can't wait

Only two hours and forty-eight minutes to go.

Madison closed her file and powered down her laptop. She had to start getting ready.

It was warm, even for September, and sunny. Madison guessed it would probably be one of the last real summer days before fall swept in with its cool breezes and rain—so she wanted to wear something summery and fun. Besides, there was no point in getting super dressed up just to go bowling. She selected a red Hello Kitty T-shirt and her jeans.

But then she thought about the fact that Hart Jones was going to be at the party. She didn't just want to wear a pair of grunged-out jeans. She went back into her closet and picked out a pair of blue-and-white-striped capris and a blue top that just grazed the top of her pants. It wasn't a belly shirt (Mom didn't like those), but it was better than a regular T-shirt.

Madison slid her feet into her favorite pair of clogs and tucked some low socks into her bag to wear inside the rented bowling-alley shoes. She ran a brush through her hair and slicked on some strawberry-kiwi-smooch lip gloss. Then she gave her armpits a sniff to make sure they weren't stinky.

All clear. There. She was ready. Almost.

She still had to wrap her gifts.

Madison walked to the hall closet and pulled out a roll of gold-foil paper and some royal-blue ribbon. She decided to wrap Chet's gift first. Madison knew he was seriously into basketball, and he liked computers a lot. So, inspired by the disk of screen savers that Mrs. Wing had given to her, Madison had picked out a screen-saver disk of NBA superstars for Chet. Well, Mom had picked it up in the software section at Stationery Barn.

Once that was wrapped, Madison went to her desk and pulled out Fiona's gift. Madison had decorated an old cigar box with a collage of words and pictures from magazines. She had wanted to use photographs of Fiona, but Fiona hadn't lived in Far Hills very long, so Madison didn't have a gazillion pictures of her as she did of Aimee or Egg. Instead, Madison had found magazine pictures of Mia Hamm and a few women from the U.S. soccer team. She'd put a bunch of words in between, like *Way to go* and *Superstar!* Once Madison had glued the art to the outside of the box, she covered it with a thin coat of special decoupage glue, so that everything stayed lacquered on. When the lid of the box was dry, she'd used a silver paint pen to write FIONA with squiggly hearts and flowers. She had also decorated the inside of the box with blue-and-white paper for sky and puffy clouds.

Before she taped the wrapping paper around the box, Madison hesitated. Would Fiona like this? Or would she be disappointed that Madison hadn't *bought* her something? She decided it would be okay and used the scissors to make a curly bow.

Dingdong!

"I've got it, Mom!" Madison shouted. The digital clock read 10:59, just about the time that Aimee was supposed to come over so Mom could drive them to the bowling alley. Madison was glad that Aimee had picked today to be on time—usually she was about ten minutes late for everything. They needed all the time they could get to set up for the party.

Madison grabbed her presents and raced down the stairs, taking them two at a time. Mom was at the bottom step, holding out a basket of cookies.

"Madison, hold these while I look for my car keys?" Mom asked. "Tell Aimee I'll be ready in a sec."

"Sure thing," Madison said. She put the basket of cookies over her arm and pulled open the door. "Hi, Aim—"

Madison stopped. She stared, jaw wide open. The person standing on her doorstep wasn't Aimee.

"Fiona?"

"Hi, Maddie," Fiona said, stepping into the front hall. "I'm sorry, I just *had* to come over. My parents are driving me nuts!" Fiona planted her hands on her hips. "My mom is fluttering around the house,

131

cleaning it from top to bottom, as though she's expecting a hundred people to come over, or something, even though she'll have all day to do that because . . . guess what! She isn't even coming with us to see these friends of Dad's! Can you believe it? My own mother is ditching her only two children *on our birthday*! She keeps saying that we'll have a special dinner when we get back, but I'm like—*why* are we even going in the first place? And Dad keeps freaking out about my shoes. For some reason, he won't let me wear sandals—he keeps saying that I have to wear shoes *with* socks. I mean, what's that all about? Are his college friends afraid of feet, or something?"

Fiona finally stopped talking and noticed the gifts in Madison's hand. "Hey . . ." she said, "are those for me?"

Madison's throat went dry. "Uh . . . uh . . ." she said. "I'm going to a party."

"You didn't tell me. Whose party?" Fiona asked.

"Well . . ." Madison said. "It's actually my mom who's going to the party. A friend from Budge Films. I'm just going with her."

"I can't believe that *you're* going to a party, and I'm not—on *my* birthday!" Fiona cried. "This is so unfair!" She checked her watch. "You'll have to tell me all about it later. I'd better get back home. Dad is totally freaking out that we have to leave *exactly on time*. My parents only let me come over here because I told then that I had to return this," she said, holding up a book on HTML that she'd borrowed from Madison to use for the Web page. "I know you don't really need it right now, but I had to get out of there. Anyway, I'll just leave it on the table, since your hands are full. E-mail when you get back, and we'll plan something fun with Aimee for tomorrow. See you!"

Madison was still standing there, openmouthed, as Fiona waved and walked out the front door.

Whew. She couldn't believe it. Fiona *still* had no clue about the surprise party? How could Madison have escaped that one?

"Where's Aimee?" Mom asked, walking into the front hall.

"That wasn't Aimee," Madison said. "It was Fiona."

Mom's eyes grew round. "Oh, no. What did you say? Did she—"

"Let's put it this way, Mom," she said, grinning. "Fiona is never going to work for the FBI . . . although she might make it into the space academy. She didn't even think it was for her. I told her I was going to some party with YOU."

"Very fast thinking, honey bear," Mom said.

The bell dinged again and they both jumped. Mom looked through the peephole. "It's okay," she said. "It's the real Aimee this time."

"Hi!" Aimee sang when Mom pulled open the

door. She was holding a big flat box tied with colorful ribbon. "Oh my God, I think I just saw Fiona walking down the street. I ducked behind a bush so she wouldn't see me. Was she *here*?"

Madison giggled. "You'll never believe what just happened." She filled Aimee in on Fiona's visit as they walked to the car.

Aimee howled with laughter. "You're kidding!" she said when Madison had finished her story. "That's classic. Fiona is the world's easiest person to throw a surprise party for."

"Tell me about it," Madison agreed. She and Aimee climbed into the backseat, because the twin cakes were riding shotgun.

"All set, girls?" Mom asked as she fastened her seat belt.

"As ready as we'll ever be," Madison said.

"Let's par-tay!" Aimee squealed.

It was a short drive to the bowling alley, but Madison and Aimee had a good laugh over the *long* drive Fiona and Chet would be taking. When they arrived, Mrs. Waters waved them over to the two center lanes, where she had already tied bunches of white and silver balloons.

"The pizzas are on their way," Mrs. Waters said as Aimee, Madison, and Mom walked up. "It's certainly starting to look like a party around here!"

"Now all we need are some guests," Madison joked.

"Should I bring in the cakes?" Mom asked Mrs. Waters.

"Actually, Fran, would you mind taking them over to our house?" Mrs. Waters replied. "That's where we'll cut the cakes and open gifts. My sister is there—she'll let you in."

"But I thought your family lived too far away to come for Chet and Fiona's birthday?" Aimee said.

"It's a surprise party, right?" Mrs. Waters said with a smile. "She flew in last night and stayed at a hotel."

"I'll see you girls later," Mom said, kissing Madison's cheek. "Have fun!"

"Bye, Mom," Madison called.

"Is there anything we can do to help?" Aimee asked Mrs. Waters.

Mrs. Waters pointed to some crepe paper lying on a chair. "Would you mind hanging the streamers?" she asked.

"No problem," Madison said. For the next half-hour, she and Aimee hung streamers and rearranged balloons until the lanes looked absolutely perfect. Then they went to get their bowling shoes. When they walked up to the counter, Lindsay Frost was standing there.

"Hi!" Lindsay bubbled. She was shy and usually kind of quiet, but today she looked and sounded like a real party girl. "I'm so happy to see you guys. I just love bowling."

"Same here," Madison said, trading in her clogs for a pair of bowling shoes.

"Although, the shoes aren't the greatest fashion statement," Aimee said with a grin. Her pair was brown and orange and covered in gross scuff marks.

"I know," Lindsay agreed. "That's why I got my own." She held out her right foot to show off a pair of cool, green shoes. "My family goes bowling a lot," she said, in response to Madison's surprised look. "I have my own ball, too," she added, holding up a green bag.

"Your own ball? That's hardcore," Aimee said.

"I hope she's on our team," Madison whispered to Aimee as they followed Lindsay back to the lanes.

Madison sat down to put on her shoes, just as Lance and Ben walked up.

"Hey, Maddie," Lance said, jumping over the back of the chairs to sit next to Madison. "Are you ready to rock and bowl?"

"I don't exactly have all the moves," Madison admitted.

"Bowling is all about angles," Ben said in his typical, know-it-all voice. "If you strike the first pin at the right angle, all the rest will fall."

"Listen, Math Man," Lance replied, "I'm happy if I can just keep my ball out of the gutter."

"Same here," Madison agreed. She wasn't a very good bowler, but, for some reason, that didn't bother her at all. Bowling was super fun, even when she was the mayor of Gutterball City.

Egg, Drew, and Dan were the next to arrive. Dan and Drew came right over, but Egg sort of hung back, pretending to take a really long time to pick out a bowling ball. Madison tried to catch his eye, but he didn't look up at her. *Grrr.* Did he have to be such a pain—even at Chet and Fiona's birthday party?

Daisy and Suresh arrived next, and Madison took a quick look at her watch. It was almost twelve-thirty. Fiona and Chet would be there within minutes, and there were still a few people missing! Where were Ivy and her drones? Even more important, where was Hart? Madison chewed on a fingernail, suddenly worried that he'd changed his mind about coming.

"Okay, everyone, you can start now," Ivy said as she walked over, followed by Phony Joanie and Rose Thorn, of course. Madison rolled her eyes.

Drew cracked up at the sight of her. "Um, Ivy . . . what are you wearing?"

Ivy folded her arms across her chest. "Duh. It's a miniskirt. What's the matter—you've never seen one before?"

"It's from Paris," Rose put in, which made Madison want to barf.

"Yeah," Drew went on. "Well . . . good luck with that."

"You can get your shoes over there," Madison said, pointing to the counter.

"I'm not taking these off," Ivy said, pointing to her strappy platforms.

Just then, the front door opened and Hart Jones came running into the bowling alley, his brown hair flying. Madison's heart nearly leaped out of her chest. When Hart saw everyone, he hurried over. "You guys, they're coming!" he shouted. "They almost saw me in the parking lot!"

"Get down, everyone," Mrs. Waters called. "We'll shout 'Surprise' on the count of three."

Hart hurried over. "Hey, Finnster—" he started to say.

But Ivy grabbed his arm.

"Hart, you just have to help me find a place to hide," she said, batting her eyelashes at him.

Now Madison *really* wanted to barf.

"Uh—just crouch down a little," Hart told Ivy. "Behind these chairs."

Everyone else crouched down, too. Madison heard a whirring noise as the electronic door swept open.

"We're meeting your college friends at a bowling alley?" she heard Fiona's voice ask. "That is so weird."

"One," Madison whispered. "Two. Three!"

"Surprise!" everyone yelled.

"Oh, my gosh!" Fiona said.

Chet's mouth hung open. It was the first time that Madison had ever seen him with nothing to say.

"I don't believe this!" Fiona went on. "A party? Dad!" She gave Mr. Waters a playful swat on the arm. "You tricked us!" Mrs. Waters gave her a big hug as Fiona started to laugh. "Mom! I can't believe you!"

Chet was still speechless. Egg walked over and gave him a high-five. Chet knocked fists with Drew, Lance, Suresh, and Hart, too, but he still couldn't speak. He just shook his head, grinning from ear to ear.

Everyone was laughing.

Fiona rushed over to Madison. "Maddie—did you know about this?"

Madison smirked. "Yes. Aimee and I helped your mom plan the whole thing."

"You did?" Fiona's eyes were huge. "But . . . how did you keep it a secret?"

Aimee and Madison looked at each other, grinning. "Actually," Madison said, "it wasn't really that hard."

"You guys are the absolute best!" Fiona said, sweeping her two BFFs into a huge hug.

Chet jumped onto a chair and held his hands in the air. Madison was glad to see that he had finally thought of something to say.

"Hey, everybody," Chet shouted. "Let the games begin!"

Chapter 12

"Okay," Aimee said, holding up a baseball cap full of little white slips of paper. "It's time to pick teams!"

"Who picks first?" Fiona asked.

"I'm older by three minutes," Chet said. "I pick first."

Fiona rolled her eyes. "What-ever."

Chet dug his hand into the hat Aimee was holding and pulled out a slip of paper. "Drew," he read. "All right!" Drew jogged over and gave Chet a nudge.

Then it was Fiona's turn. She chose her slip of paper and smiled. "Madison!" she shouted.

Madison hurried over and gave Fiona a hug. They both looked over at Aimee. One more pick and she'd be on their team, too.

But when Chet dug his hand into the hat, *he* pulled out Aimee's name.

"Bummer," Madison thought. Aimee looked a

little disappointed, too, but she walked over and stood next to Drew.

When Fiona read the name on the next slip of paper, her face lit up. "Egg," she said.

Egg—on my team? Madison wanted to slink away when he came over and stood on the other side of Fiona. He still hadn't spoken to Madison yet since arriving at the bowling lanes. Please don't let us get Ivy, too, Madison begged silently.

Chet and Fiona continued to take turns. Chet ended up with Drew, Aimee, Suresh, Daisy, Poison Ivy (thankfully), Lance, and Dan on his team. Fiona got Madison, Ben, Phony Joanie, Rose Thorn, Lindsay, and Hart. Despite the presence of the drones on her team, Madison was excited. She'd rather have them than Ivy herself. Besides, Lindsay was on the team, and she was practically a professional bowler. And Hart, too.

"Who wants to keep score for us?" Fiona asked.

"I will," Hart volunteered. He sat down at the scoring swivel chair.

"I'll keep score for *our* team," Ivy told Chet, sliding into the seat next to Hart. Ben looked disappointed, of course, since he was the math whiz and had been hoping to be scorekeeper.

Ivy stared at the buttons on the little table in front of her; and then looked up at the TV screen mounted from the ceiling. "How do you work this thing?" she asked aloud.

Hart punched his own and then Fiona's initials

into the electronic scorekeeper. "Okay, Finnster," he called out. "What's your middle name?"

Madison blushed. "Francesca," she said.

"Cool name," Hart said. When he smiled, the cute dimple in his left cheek showed.

Madison's legs turned to Jell-O as Hart typed "MFF" into the keyboard, and her initials popped up on the screen overhead.

"Let's go get a bowling ball," Fiona said. Madison nodded.

There were racks and racks of balls in front of the concession stand. Madison picked up a funky, orange, marbleized ball, but was disappointed to find that it was way too heavy. She ended up with a yellow one, while Fiona picked hot pink.

The bowling alley had started to fill up by one o'clock, and all around them the air was filled with the low rumble of balls rolling over smooth wood, and the hollow, knocking sound of pins falling. Madison spotted Dan, Ben, and Drew at the jukebox, and a moment later, an Elvis song started blasting through the speakers.

"Couldn't you guys find something from this millennium?" Chet shouted.

"All they have are oldies," Drew said as he trotted back to the lanes. "Besides, Dan loves Elvis."

"He's the king," Dan agreed.

Madison laughed. Somehow, music from the fifties went well with bowling.

"All right," Hart said as Madison put her ball in the conveyor belt that divided the lanes between the two teams. "Fiona, you're up first."

Fiona held her ball at chest level and surveyed the lane. Then she took a deep breath, stepped forward, and released the ball. It zoomed straight . . . into the gutter.

"Oh, no!" Fiona said as the electronic scoreboard played a dismal little tune and flashed GUTTER BALL! across the screen. "Like it wasn't embarrassing enough without the added humiliation of *that*?"

"Ha-ha!" Chet laughed and pointed at his sister. "Watch and learn," he said. He bowled the ball, which veered slightly to the right. "Go to the left!" Chet shouted. "Left, left, left!" The ball skirted the edge of the gutter, but rolled slightly right at the last moment, knocking down two pins. "All right!" Chet shouted. "Two!"

"Two?" Ivy looked disgusted as the score popped up on the screen and the scoreboard chirped a happy tune. "Well, at least we're winning."

Fiona's ball popped up onto the conveyor belt, and she took her second turn. She got another gutter ball. She gave a little half-laugh, half-groan as the scoreboard played "Taps." "I guess I haven't discovered my hidden talent," Fiona said, flopping into her chair. "Next time I bowl, maybe I should put up the gutter guards."

Chet knocked down three more pins on his next

143

turn. He did a victory dance around the lane.

Hart was up next for Fiona's team. He knocked down eight pins on his first try and then got a spare. Everyone on the team stood up and cheered as the scoreboard erupted into electronic fireworks.

"Way to go, cuz!" Drew called from Chet's team. "But we'll get you back!"

"Go, Hart! Go, Hart!" Egg started a chant. Everyone joined, including Madison.

Egg went next, knocking down nine pins in two turns. Madison was impressed. As the rest of the team congratulated him, he looked right at Madison. Quickly, she gave him a thumbs-up, and he flashed her a goofy half-smile in return.

"Madison, you're up," Rose Thorn called.

Madison grabbed her yellow ball, and walked to the line. She could practically feel everyone's eyes on her as she rolled the ball. It went straight into the gutter, just like Fiona's ball.

"Thank goodness!" Fiona called. "Now I don't feel so bad!"

Madison laughed as the electronic guards went up at the end of the lane. Seeing that made her BFF feel even better. Luckily, Madison didn't mind bowling gutter balls—luckily, because she threw another one a moment later.

Madison felt a little guilty that her score would bring the team down, but Lindsay Frost was up next. She pulled her green ball off the conveyor belt and bowled a strike. Everyone ran up to congratulate her.

Phony Joanie turned out to be a pretty good bowler, too. She knocked down eight pins.

"Wow," Madison said as Joan returned to her seat. "How did you do that?"

"You just have to keep your arm straight," Joan replied. "And look at the pins, not the ball."

Madison nodded. She hadn't actually expected an answer like that from Phony Joanie.

Aimee got up to bowl next for Chet's team. Madison grinned as her friend took three large leaps, then gracefully swung the ball away from her. It looked like a choreographed dance routine, but—amazingly—it knocked down six pins.

Madison clapped even though Aimee was on the other team. "Way to go, Aim!" she said.

On Chet's team, it was Ivy's turn. Gingerly, Ivy picked up a ball, and tottered up to the line in her platforms. She took a step forward, then started to bend over to roll her ball . . . but at the last minute, she straightened up and turned around. Her face was bright red—and Madison knew why. If Ivy had leaned over any further in the short skirt she was wearing, everyone at the party would have gotten a good look at her backside.

"I see London, I see France. . . ." Chet called out.

"I see Ivy's—" Egg started to say.

"SHUT UP!" Ivy yelled so loud her face got all

puffy. Madison knew that look. She'd been on the receiving end of it too many times.

Ivy smoothed her miniskirt back down again and pressed her lips together as she turned back to face the lane. Without bending over, Ivy dropped the ball with a thud. It rolled a few feet, and fell into the gutter.

And it stopped.

Ivy crossed her arms and just stood there. Mrs. Waters found an attendant to walk into the lane and free the bowling ball. He reset the machine, and then pointed to Ivy's shoes.

"You can't wear those shoes on the lane surface," he said. "Sorry. I'd be happy to bring you some bowling shoes. What size do you wear?"

"Oh, that's okay," Ivy said, uncrossing her arms and acting sugar-sweet. "I think I sprained my finger when I bowled that last one. I should probably just sit out for a while."

"Say what?" Chet cried. The kids on his team rushed over.

Mrs. Waters picked up Ivy's hand and examined her fingers. "Everything looks okay. . . ." she said. "Can you bend them? Should I bring you some ice?"

"Oh, yes," Ivy replied sweetly. "Thank you so much."

Madison bit back a sarcastic comment. It was so obvious that Ivy just didn't want to ruin her outfit or flash everyone her stupid underwear. Did she have to be so fake about everything?

Mrs. Waters brought Ivy a cup of ice while everyone else continued with the game. Daisy bowled a spare, Ben got a perfect ten, and Rose knocked down seven pins. Chet's team was ahead.

A delicious smell wafted past Madison's nose, and when she turned, she saw a man holding a stack of four pizzas. Madison and Aimee hurried to help Mrs. Waters set up the food on the large table against the wall. A pile of brightly wrapped presents decorated one table. Madison pulled the plastic off a stack of cups and began filling a few with ice from the cooler Mrs. Waters had brought. After washing her hands, Aimee served slices of pizza onto plates.

"I really can't thank you girls enough," Mrs. Waters said. "I think this party is going wonderfully."

"It's a lot of fun, Mrs. Waters," Madison said. "We were glad to help."

"Absolutely," Aimee agreed. "And I love bowling, even if I stink at it."

"You definitely have a unique technique," Madison told her.

Suresh and Drew wandered over and grabbed slices of pizza and sat down. Fiona ran up and gave Madison a huge hug from behind. "You guys, I am having the best time!" she exclaimed. "This is the best birthday ever."

"Oh, come on," Aimee said, laughing.

"No," Fiona shook her head. "I really mean it. The best. Ever."

The friends looked at one another a moment,

then dove into a group hug. The craziness of the past week was totally worth it, Madison thought, if she could help make her friend this happy.

"And the party's only just beginning!" Madison shouted.

The bowling match was close, but in the end, Fiona's team won by five points, thanks to the Princess of Strikes, Lindsay Frost. Once everyone had finished bowling and pigging out on pizza, they headed out to the parking lot, where Mr. and Mrs. Waters, Señora Diaz, and Mrs. Gillespie were waiting in their minivans to take everyone over to the Waterses' house. Madison couldn't believe how much organization it took to plan a surprise party—and Mrs. Waters had really thought of everything.

When the convoy of minivans pulled up in front of the Waterses' old Victorian house, everyone tumbled out onto the sidewalk. Chet and Fiona were headed up the flagstone path when the front door to their house flew open.

"Aunt Sheila?" Chet cried. "Whoa!"

Chet and Fiona raced each other up the steps to say hello. Aunt Sheila squeezed her niece and nephew until they were gasping for air.

Madison and the other kids hung back, not wanting to spoil the moment.

"I'm so glad you're here!" Fiona said. "Come and meet my friends!"

The party guests stood in a semicircle on the front lawn while Fiona and Chet introduced their aunt to everyone. Aunt Sheila had caramel-colored skin and long, dark hair just like Mrs. Waters's.

"Okay, troops! Let's go inside for cake!" Mrs. Waters said, clapping her hands. The group hustled through the door.

When everyone was settled into the couch and on the floor of the living room, Mrs. Waters turned out the lights so everyone could sing "Happy Birthday." Then she and Aunt Sheila came into the room with the dessert.

"Two cakes?" Chet howled. "Wahoo! We never got that before."

"For once, we didn't have to fight over who gets to blow out the candles," Fiona said.

"Mmmm. This cake is awesome!" Dan said, taking a big forkful of chocolate frosting. Dan always got to the food first.

"I can't believe you guys made this," Chet said to Madison and Aimee, sounding impressed.

After the cakes were sliced, Fiona and Chet opened presents. Chet tore the wrapping off each of his gifts, but Fiona went more slowly, pulling off ribbon and placing it aside, then opening the paper as though she didn't want to tear it.

Madison rocked from foot to foot as she watched them open all the gifts. Chet really liked the screen savers Madison had got him. "I saw this in the store!" he said when he unwrapped it. "Thanks, Maddie."

But Fiona's reaction was even better. When she pulled the paper off, Fiona just stared at Madison's collage box for a long time, examining it from every angle, taking in each and every picture and word. Then she opened it, and smiled when she saw the clouds.

"Maddie, I love it," Fiona said quietly.

"Pass it around, so everyone can look at it," Hart said.

Madison beamed. She knew a store-bought gift wouldn't have gotten that reaction.

"Nice job, Madison," Ivy said as she passed the box to the next person.

Madison stared at her enemy. Was Ivy being sarcastic? Was it possible that Poison Ivy had just given her—Madison Finn—a compliment? Maybe Ivy still had a nice streak inside of her somewhere?

When Egg looked at the box, he didn't make one of his usual obnoxious remarks. He just smiled. So Madison smiled back. Although they hadn't exchanged two words today, things seemed better with Egg. Once the party was over, she could apologize and they'd be best friends again—she hoped.

Madison sank back onto the living room couch, happily squeezed between Aimee and the armrest. She took a forkful of chocolate cake. It *was* yummy.

"We did a good job," Aimee whispered. "Didn't we?"

Madison looked up at Fiona, who was laughing at something Chet had said. Both twins couldn't stop smiling and joking around. Neither twin could stop this party.

On top of Fiona's collage box, Madison had pasted the words *love to party with my pals.* She'd found it in some teen magazine. Right now, those words felt truer than true.

This was one party that no one would soon forget.

Chapter 13

"Maddie! Phone!" Mom yelled. She was standing in the hallway holding the portable phone.

Groaning, Madison rolled over and looked at her alarm clock. Who in the world would be calling at nine o'clock on a Sunday morning? She rolled out from under the blankets, bleary-eyed, and tugged on her monkey slippers. Mom handed her the phone.

"Hello?" Madison croaked.

"Maddie!" It was Fiona. "I'm not waking you up, am I?"

"Uh—no, no," Madison lied, rubbing her eyes. She climbed back onto her bed and plumped her pillow against the headboard. Phin moved into her lap to snuggle. "What's up, Fiona?"

"I just wanted to call and say thank you for

everything. The party was such a surprise," Fiona chirped. "I had so much fun!"

"I'm glad," Madison said, stroking Phin's silky ear. "I had a great time, too."

"The cakes were awesome—I can't believe that you and Aimee actually made two of them," Fiona went on. "And I love, love, love my box, Maddie. I put it on my dresser, so I can look at it every day."

"It was no big deal," Madison said.

"No big deal?" Fiona squealed. "Even Chet had a good time—and we never like the same things. But we think it was our nicest birthday ever."

Madison giggled. "When I checked my e-mail last night, Chet had sent me a note."

There was a beat of silence. "You're kidding," Fiona said.

"No lie," Madison said. "He said thanks for the screen savers. I guess he was in the middle of down-loading them onto the computer."

"Now, *that's* a surprise!" Fiona laughed. "I have to admit that my brother can sometimes be a pretty good guy, even if he is a big pain in the butt."

"I guess you can keep him," Madison said.

Fiona snorted. "Not like I have a choice. Wow! It actually is possible to have a twin birthday that isn't a total drag. Who knew?"

"So—" Madison said, fighting back a yawn, "what are you guys up to today?"

"We're going to the aquarium with my aunt

Sheila," Fiona said. "That's part of the reason I called. I know that I said you and Aimee and I would hang out together today, but—"

"No problem," Madison said. "I totally understand. Besides, Aimee said that she might have to help out her dad at the cyber café, so this actually works out."

"Sorry," Fiona replied. "What about you?"

"I'm not really doing anything," Madison said honestly. "I'm going to do some homework and chill out with Phin, maybe rent a video."

"Sounds good—oh, wait, hold on a second." Madison heard Fiona shout, "I'm coming!" then she put the receiver back to her mouth. "Listen, my family is about to leave. I'll call or e-mail you later, okay?"

"Sure," Madison said. "Have fun."

"Bye."

Madison clicked off the phone, closed her eyes, and stretched her legs out on the bed. Phin yawned and slid onto the mattress from her lap. He licked his lips. "I feel the same way," Madison said. "Why am I so tired?"

Madison got up out of the bed and pulled a sweatshirt on over her pajamas. "We have a lot to catch up on, Phinnie," she said aloud. Maybe today was a good day to reorganize her computer files?

Madison padded over to her desk and booted up her laptop.

Surprises

Sometimes, I get so caught up in doing things that I completely forget what I'm doing them for.

1. Fiona's party. I got so tied up in who to invite and who not to invite, what food to serve, and what kind of cake to bake, that I totally forgot that the party was supposed to make Fiona happy. And I NEVER thought about whether it would make Chet happy or not. But it did. Way happy. And everyone else had a good time, too—including me.

2. The contest Web page. Fiona and I worked so hard, and once we turned it in, I was frustrated that it didn't come out perfect and that it didn't have all those sounds and flashy graphics. But we didn't have that much time, and we did a really good job, considering. Why be bummed? The whole point was to do it and be proud about it, right?

3. The stuff with Egg and Dad and being mad. I haven't totally been myself lately. Was it because Egg didn't pick me as his Web page partner? That doesn't make any sense. I can't stay mad at someone I've known forever. Just because he picked Chet instead of me? And when I blew up at Dad the other night—that was bad. He was only trying to help me. I mean, what was that argument *for*?

Rude Awakening: This week I've managed to make it through thick . . . and twin. LOL. But no matter how difficult things seem . . . they always work out in the end, right? Gramma Helen says so. I keep telling myself that. All I have to do is say I'm sorry. That can't be so hard, can it?

Madison closed the file and went into bigfishbowl.com, hoping that Bigwheels would be logged on. But she was nowhere to be found.

From: MadFinn
To: Bigwheels
Subject: LTNW!
Date: Sun 1 Oct 10:36 AM

Hey! Haven't had an e-msg from you in a while. How's school? Life? Everything? Do u go in bigfishbowl chat rooms n e more?

The Web page and Fiona's surprise party worked out great. Whew!

And remember Hart? When he saw the birthday gift I gave Fiona, he said it was cool . . . and then he told me that I was a good bowler, too. What does *that* mean? Is that one for the Random Compliment Dept., or

what? (Especially because, hel-lo,
my bowling is lame-o). But that's
another story, LOL.

Write back because I MISS U!!!

Yours till the gutter balls,

MadFinn

BTW, a big, fat THANK YOU for your
help with the Web page!! My teacher
loved it! Your homework links were
the best ones.

"Honey bear?"

Mom's voice behind her made Madison jump.

"Mom!" she cried. "I hate it when you sneak up on me like that!" Madison was still sleepy.

Mom grinned and shook her head. "I've been calling you for the last five minutes," Mom said. "It looks like you were just too lost in cyberspace to hear me."

"Sorry," Madison said, yawning again.

"Your dad is on the phone," Mom said. "Pick up, okay?"

Madison dove for the cordless and flopped onto her bed. "Thanks, Mom!" She clicked the talk button. "Dad?"

"Hi, Maddie," Dad said.

"Where are you?" Madison asked breathlessly. "When are you coming home?" There was so much she wanted to say—including, *I'm sorry*, for the other night at Bombay Palace.

"I'm at home," Dad said. "Actually, I was wondering if I could come over. I have an idea about something we can do together, just the two of us."

"What is it?" Madison was practically squealing. "Oh, come over, Dad. Come over right away. What's your idea?"

"I was thinking we could go back and see the puppies again."

Madison grinned. "The puppies! Oh, yes!"

"I'll come by in twenty minutes," Dad said. "Okay?"

"I love you, Dad," she said.

"I love you more," Dad said.

Madison jumped into a pair of jeans and pulled on a thin sweater. The temperature had dropped ten degrees from the day before. "Mom!" she called, hurrying into Mom's office, where Mom was flipping through some notes on a yellow legal pad. "I'm going to hang out with Dad today, okay?"

"Of course, honey bear," Mom said. "I'll be working, anyway."

"Great!" Madison headed downstairs and dashed into the kitchen for some juice and toast. She tossed a dog chew toy at Phinnie, since he was following her around. As she was rinsing her plate in the sink, the doorbell rang.

"Bye, Mom!" Madison cried. "Bye, Phinnie," she added, giving him a smooch on the top of his head.

"Have fun!" Mom yelled back.

Madison ran to the door and pulled it open.

"Hi, sweetie," Dad said. Phin barked and wiggled at Dad's feet. "Hey to you, too, Phinnie. Sorry I'm taking Maddie away for the afternoon."

"Rowrooo!" Phin howled.

"Oh, Phin," Madison said, giving him a pat. "We're just going to see some puppies—that's all. I'll be back soon."

Phin started to chase his tail as Madison and Dad closed the door. Madison looked back twice on the walk down to the car and saw Phin perched in the window, watching them.

"I guess little Phin is a bit jealous of the puppies, huh? Maybe we should bring him a little treat, so he knows he's still number one."

Madison smiled. That was just like Dad. Even though he didn't live with them anymore, he hadn't forgotten about the important stuff. He still worried about feelings—even Phin's.

On the way to the clinic, Madison edged over in the seat, closer to Dad. "Listen," she said, "there's something I need to tell you, Dad."

Dad gripped the steering wheel and slowed the car down a little.

"There's something I need to tell you, too, Maddie," he said.

Madison took a deep breath. Should she say what she had to say—or let Dad speak?

"Okay, you first," Madison said.

Dad cleared his throat and stared straight ahead while he spoke. He had to keep his eyes on the road.

"Sometimes it's hard for a parent to realize that their child is growing up," Dad said slowly. "It's just that I remember what you were like when you were a little girl. I took care of you—did everything for you. And sometimes I forget that you don't need me to solve all of your problems for you anymore. You're growing up, Maddie. And since the divorce, I just—"

Dad pulled the car over. They sat there in silence for a moment.

"Maddie, I'm sorry that I pressured you about Egg the other night. I know that's why you got upset with me. I also know you'll work out your problems with him on your own. You don't need my help."

Madison's vision blurred, and she had to blink hard to clear the tears from her eyes. "Oh, Dad." She leaned over and gave him a huge hug. Her throat was tight, but she knew that she had to go on. "I do need your help . . . even if I sometimes act like I don't. I am so sorry, too."

Dad's sad smile brightened. "Well, how about this? The next time you want advice on something, you can just ask, and I'll help. Then we won't get our signals crossed."

"It's a deal," Madison said. She felt as though a huge weight had just been lifted off her chest. Even though she'd always known that Dad wouldn't be mad at her forever, it was nice to know that he wasn't mad at her right now.

"So," Dad said as he started the car again and eased it into the street. "How did the Web page go? Did you win the contest?"

"The results aren't in yet," Madison said. "Although Mrs. Wing says they turn around the judging over the weekend. It's sponsored by this big company called Web-tastic Media Partners, and they have a team of judges, so . . . who knows?"

She stared out the window as the trees and sidewalk whizzed by.

"I don't think we really have a chance of winning, Dad. You know that, right?" Madison said.

"Maddie!" Dad said. "I think you should just wait and see. How did you like building the page? Do you think you're interested in a career with computers? It can be a lot of fun," he added, waggling his eyebrows. "*Tech* it from me."

Madison laughed at the bad pun. "Oh, Dad," she said. "Yeah, I had fun, but I don't know if I want that to be my job. I think I might like to be a vet."

Madison thought again about Fleet's puppies. She was excited to see how much they'd grown.

Dad nodded. "Being a veterinarian is a lot of work," he said.

"Yeah," Madison agreed as she looked out the windshield at the ribbon of road unwinding before her. "I know."

"But I know you can do it, Maddie," Dad went on. "You can do whatever you put your mind to, Madison Finn."

Madison put her hand gently on her father's arm. He looked over and smiled.

"Thanks, Dad," she said warmly. She didn't say "Thanks for everything," but that was what she meant.

Dad patted her hand. "You're welcome," he said. And Madison knew by the sound of his voice that he meant *for everything*, too.

Chapter 14

"Hey, Maddie!" Fiona was standing with Aimee at her locker, waving frantically.

"Hey, guys!" Madison called. "Listen, I've got to ask Mrs. Wing something, I'll be back in a minute, okay?"

"We'll be here," Aimee promised, pulling her heavy Spanish book from her locker. "Until the first bell rings, anyway."

Madison scurried to the computer lab, eager to learn the Web page contest results. Dad had made Madison promise she would find out and e-mail him about it first thing Monday morning. But when Madison pushed open the door to the computer lab, she saw that Mrs. Wing's big blue desk chair was empty.

"Hello?" Madison called softly.

Madison took a tentative step into the room, and saw that someone was standing at the back, looking up at Mrs. Wing's How to Make a Web Page bulletin board display. Madison knew exactly who it was, with his shirt untucked, his head tilted at a familiar angle.

Egg.

She hesitated only a moment before walking over and standing beside him. For a moment, neither one of them spoke.

"The pages look good, right?" Egg said.

"Yeah." Madison noticed that the printout of her and Fiona's page was at the center of the display, right beside Egg and Chet's page. "Your page is very cool, with that *Star Wars* theme and all."

Egg dug his hands into his pockets. "Thanks," he said. "Actually, Maddie, I think yours is better. I think I'm going to copy down a couple of your links," he admitted, giving Madison a lopsided grin. "I've got to work on that science project for Mr. Danehy."

"Oh, right," Madison said. "I've got to get started on that, too."

They stared up at the display a moment longer. Was this the right time to tell Egg how sorry she was that they had been fighting all week?

"It's hard, isn't it?" Egg said.

Madison stared at him. "Hard?"

Was he talking about making a Web page—or apologizing? The answer was the same, either way.

"Yeah," Madison said.

"It's so much work," Egg went on. "Sometimes you think it isn't worth it—that you should just give up. . . ." His voice trailed off.

"But you don't," Madison finished for him.

"Yeah." Egg looked at her, his freckles standing out against his tan skin. "I've been thinking about what you said, how you were mad because I didn't pick you as my partner."

"You have?" Madison said.

"I'm really sorry about that, Maddie," Egg said.

Madison winced. "Egg—I'm so sorry about that, too," she said. "It just . . . hurt my feelings, and then I started yelling and . . . I'm sorrier than sorry."

Egg raised his eyebrows. "Well, don't get all carried away."

Madison looked down at the floor.

"The thing is . . ." Egg said. "You were right."

Madison gaped at him. "I was?"

"Yeah." Egg ran a hand nervously through his hair. "Don't tell Chet this, but—" He glanced nervously over his shoulder. "You would have made a much cooler partner."

"Really?" Madison smiled.

Egg nodded. "Really. He just wanted to goof off a lot, you know?"

"We would have made a good team," Madison agreed.

Egg shrugged. "Next time," he said. "I promise."

"It's a deal," Madison replied.

"You know, Maddie," Egg went on, staring at the floor. "You're, like, my best friend who is a girl. But, in a lot of ways, you're also my best *any* friend."

Madison felt her chest grow tight. She knew that it hadn't been easy for Egg to say that. The words made Madison so happy that she wanted to throw her arms around Egg and give him a big hug. But she knew that would only embarrass him. Instead, she just said, "Me, too."

Just then, the door swung open and Mrs. Wing walked in. "Oh, hi," she said with a smile. "I didn't realize anyone was in here."

"We were just looking at the display, Mrs. Wing," Egg said formally. "This was a really cool contest."

"Mrs. Wing," Madison said, "my dad was wondering when the results would be in."

"The judges should be notifying the school pretty soon," Mrs. Wing said. "Could be this morning—could be Friday morning. They've been judging all weekend, I think."

"Do you think any of us have a chance at winning?" Egg wanted to know.

Mrs. Wing sighed. "I really don't know, Walter," Mrs. Wing admitted. "When I submitted Web pages for our school, the woman told me that they had already received over four thousand other entries."

Egg let out a low whistle. "Four *thousand*?"

Mrs. Wing nodded and tucked a stray strand of

dark hair behind her ear. "But the important thing is that you *tried*. I'm very proud of what your two teams, in particular, did."

Suddenly, the loudspeaker at the front of the room shrieked, then crackled. "Good morning, everyone," said the voice of Mrs. Goode, the assistant principal. "This is an announcement to inform everyone that there will be no homeroom this morning for the seventh grade. . . ."

A cheer went up in the hallway.

"Instead," Mrs. Goode went on, oblivious to the noise, "all seventh-grade students should proceed directly to the auditorium, where there will be a presentation about our new fire-drill procedures." Groans came from the hall. "Thank you."

The bell rang.

"I'll see you in the auditorium," Mrs. Wing said.

Madison and Egg said good-bye and walked into the hall.

"Can you believe that? Why do teachers always tell you that it's important to *try*?" Egg griped to Madison as they joined the river of students that rolled toward the auditorium. "When I enter a contest, I want to win."

Madison hiked her book bag up higher onto her shoulder. She was proud of their Web page, whether it won or not. "Come on, Egg, will you *really* be disappointed if you don't win?"

"Duh," Egg said, rolling his eyes. "Yeah!"

Madison laughed.

"Egg! Maddie!"

Madison looked over and saw Aimee leaning by her locker, standing next to Fiona, Chet, and Drew. "I thought you'd never get here," Aimee said.

"Sorry," Madison replied. "I had to wait for Mrs. Wing."

"Come on, you guys," Chet urged. "Let's hurry, so we can get seats together."

The auditorium was already packed by the time the friends walked inside, but they managed to find six seats together toward the back. Madison sat down between Egg and Aimee. Fiona was on the other side of Egg, next to Chet.

The stage was arranged with a podium and two chairs. Mr. Bernard, the principal, sat in one, and Poison Ivy sat in the other. Her legs were crossed primly, and she kept tossing her red hair over her shoulder.

"Hey, Maddie, who am I?" Egg asked, shouting to be heard over the noise of the rapidly filling auditorium. He shook his hair, as though he were in a shampoo commercial, batted his eyelashes, and pouted. "I'm president of the seventh grade!"

Madison, Aimee, and Fiona all cracked up.

Mr. Bernard walked up to the podium and tapped the microphone. A small shriek of feedback silenced the room.

"Good morning," Mr. Bernard said into the microphone. "As you may already know, the student council has spent a great deal of time reworking the fire-drill system. Here to explain the new procedures is seventh-grade president, Ivy Daly."

There was a smattering of applause as Ivy looked out at the crowd and waved.

Egg looked at Madison and waved too, pretending that he was the queen of England. Madison's shoulders shook with silent laughter. Luckily, the drones were not nearby.

"But before we do that," Mr. Bernard went on, "I'd like to make a couple of announcements. It has come to my attention that several of our students have entered a national computer Web-page design contest." He said the words *Web page* carefully, as though pronouncing something in a foreign language. "And we have just been informed that the results were tabulated over the weekend."

A murmur of surprise rippled through the auditorium, and Madison looked over at Fiona with raised eyebrows. Fiona shrugged in an "I had no idea" gesture. How had they gotten through all the entries so quickly?

"Although none of our students will be competing for the grand prize," Mr. Bernard said, "we did have two entries that took honorable mentions, one for functionality, and one for design." Mr. Bernard looked down at his notes. "Would Fiona Waters, Madison Finn, Chet Waters, and Walter Diaz please stand up and be recognized?"

A huge cheer went up from the crowd, and Chet practically jumped out of his chair, dragging Fiona with him. "Yeah!" Chet shouted, pumping his fist in the air.

Fiona looked over at Madison, giggling. "Stand up!" she whispered, gesturing wildly. "Don't leave me up here alone!"

"No way!" Madison sunk down into her seat, laughing. She was proud and embarrassed at the same time. Even though she was glad to have won an honorable mention, no way did she want to stand up and wave to everyone like Poison Ivy.

Mr. Bernard blinked out into the audience. "Er— are you standing?" he asked.

"Come on, Maddie," Egg whispered. "You have to get up."

Madison shook her head, blushing. "Forget it."

"Go on, Maddie!" Aimee urged, clapping. "Stand up!"

"I dare you," Egg said with a wicked grin. "I double-dare you."

"You double-dare me?" Madison asked with a laugh. "Then, fine!"

"On the count of three. One, two—"

"Three!" Madison popped up next to Egg and then they both immediately sat back down again, cracking up.

"You sat down first!" Madison insisted.

"You are such a total chicken," Egg countered.

Fiona slid into her seat as the applause died down. But Chet continued to smile and wave.

"Thank you, my fans!" he called. "I'll never forget all of you little people—"

Fiona yanked her brother back into his seat. "Stop embarrassing me," she hissed.

"But they love me!" Chet insisted.

Egg looked over at Madison, rolling his eyes. She giggled and put her palms to her cheeks—which were burning hot!

Even if she was slightly mortified, Madison was proud to have been able to stand up with her friends—especially Egg. She and Fiona had worked hard, and she hadn't given up, even when things got tough.

This week, Madison was a winner.

She couldn't wait to tell Dad and Bigwheels all about it.

Mad Chat Words:

1-)	Tee hee
(:-D	Blabbermouth
X-S	Completely confused
NE1	Anyone
007	Top Secret
IHNI	I have no idea
NYP	Not your problem
SB	Supposed to be
NM	Never mind
DLTBBB	Don't Let the Bed Bugs Bite
YOYO	You're on Your Own

Madison's Computer Tip

I couldn't believe it when Mrs. Waters asked Aimee and me to help her plan the surprise party for Fiona and Chet. Mostly, I was glad because it gave us a chance to write our first e-mail invitation. **Sometimes e-mail can be the most creative way to say hello—or even invite someone to a party!** I think that sending electronic invitations—e-vites—is cool, because everyone gets theirs at the same time—and can send an RSVP right away.

Visit Madison at www.madisonfinn.com